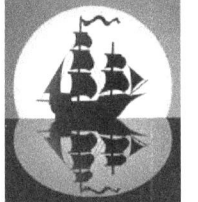

Also from Indigo Sea Press

by Carol Pearce Bjorlie

Sweet Harmony

Perfect Harmony

indigoseapress.com

Life Harmony

By

Carol Pearce Bjorlie

Sepia Books
Published by Indigo Sea Press
Winston-Salem

Sepia Books
Indigo Sea Press
302 Ricks Drive
Winston-Salem, NC 27103

This book is a work of fiction. Names, characters, locations and events are either a product of the author's imagination, fictitious or used fictitiously. Any resemblance to any event, locale or person, living or dead, is purely coincidental.

First Sepia Books edition published
January, 2016
Sepia Books, Moon Sailor and all production design are trademarks of Indigo Sea Press, used under license.

For information regarding bulk purchases of this book, digital purchase and special discounts, please contact the publisher at indigoseapress.com

Cover design by Pan Morelli

Manufactured in the United States of America
ISBN 978-1-63066-209-7

For Friends ~

Linda Andreozzi, Julie Gonner, Dorothy Cole

and Ruthie Rosauer

Chapter One

SEPTEMBER

Julie walked past Iris' desk and whispered, "Martha Rose is sitting outside the principal's office."

Iris looked up from her book. What in the world was her five-year-old sister doing outside the principal's office? She'd been in school two weeks. Iris thought she'd walk up to the teacher's desk and tell her Martha Rose was in trouble. No. That wouldn't work. Mrs. Nilsen would say her sister had to take care of herself. Mrs. Nilsen didn't know Martha Rose!

Iris went to the teacher's desk and picked up a hall pass. These cards gave students permission to leave their classroom. Mrs. Nilsen looked up from her work and smiled at Iris.

Julie and Iris had been best friends for two years. When they discovered their ninth grade teacher was to be Mrs. Nilsen, they could hardly believe it. Mrs. Nilsen, the pastor's wife, hadn't taught school for five years, and now, there she was. Mrs. Nilsen was one of Iris' favorite people in all of Harmony.

Iris hurried into the hall and ran down the wide stairs. She felt the worn wood treads through her new shoes. Sure enough, there sat Martha Rose on the bench in front of the principal's office. Her little sister's legs stuck out from the seat. She was shaking one foot in rhythm to a song. As Iris came near she heard, "You are my sunshine, my only sunshine."

Iris sat next to her sister. "What are you doing here," she asked.

Martha Rose continued to jiggle her foot and gave Iris a long look. "I punched Lily Carlson in the gut."

Iris jumped from the bench. "You did what?"

"I punched Lily Carlson in the gut. Please sit down, Iris." Martha Rose tugged on her sister's sleeve.

Iris thought to herself, imagine Martha Rose saying

'please.' Mrs. Ludvingson's summer assistance in the shrubbery classroom with Martha Rose was invaluable. They read and worked on vocabulary together. As of July, Martha Rose stopped saying, "ain't." Now, she was saying, 'please, thank you, and you're welcome.' Mrs. Ludvigson was the queen of grammar, queen of hats and scarves, and the queen of turquoise.

Iris sat down. "What did Lily do?" she asked.

"Cried," answered Martha Rose.

"I can't believe it! Mother is going to have a fit when she gets here. Martha Rose, I can't believe you'd punch anybody!"

"Lily believes it."

"Who is Lily anyway," asked Iris.

The double doors at the end of the hall opened and Iris' mother walked in. She supported Benjamin on one hip which gave her a lop-sided gait. He was seven months old. As their mother approached the bench, she locked her gaze on Martha Rose and stood in front of her. The door to the principal's office opened and out peeked Mrs. Davis' gray head.

"Mrs. Andersen," she said in her quiet voice, "You got here in a hurry."

Her mother plopped Benjamin in Iris' arms. "Would you please stay out here with Ben while Miss Davis and I have a talk?"

"We can talk right here. I'm sure you haven't heard the whole story." The principal opened her office door wider and a pale woman walked into the hall. "This is Mrs. Carlson, Lily's mother," explained Miss Davis.

Mrs. Carlson's hair was white-blonde and hung in straight wisps around her thin face. She gave Iris and her mother a weak smile, then looked at the floor.

Martha Rose stopped jiggling her foot.

Mrs. Carlson looked at Martha Rose, then said, "Young lady, you deserve a reward."

Iris' mother interrupted. "A reward? Didn't she hit your daughter in the stomach?"

Miss Davis added, "Mrs. Andersen, Lily is the youngest of

six children. The other five are boys." She nodded her head knowingly.

Mrs. Carlson leaned towards Martha Rose. Her hair made a curtain around her blue eyes. "My daughter has been bullying children since she could walk. She bullies her big brothers. They are saints. You're the first to challenge her and give her what she deserves. Thank you." She held out a tiny hand to Martha Rose who gave it a firm shake.

"You're welcome. I like Lily. May Lily come and play with me?" Martha Rose looked from her mother to Mrs. Carlson.

The two women looked at each other for the first time and began to laugh. Miss Davis chuckled.

Iris' mother wiped tears of laughter from her eyes and spoke to Mrs. Carlson, "Please, bring Lily soon and stay for a visit." She gave her hand to Mrs. Carlson. "Our family has lived in Harmony for two years, and I haven't met you. I'm Laura Ellen Andersen. This is Martha Rose," Iris' mother gestured to the child on the bench. "This is my oldest daughter, Iris, and our baby, Ben."

Mrs. Carlson backed down the hallway. "You're kind," she said wistfully, "Lily doesn't get along with other children. I don't think it would be a good idea."

Iris thought to herself, Lily has met her match. These two little girls will probably be best friends. Imagine the trouble they'll get into.

Miss Davis said, "I'll send Lily out. Mrs. Carlson, I'd like for her to stay home for two days and think about her behavior." She opened the door to her office and motioned for the occupant to come out. Iris was shocked when a sweet looking curly-haired child came out, her face blotched from crying. She walked past Martha Rose without a glance and followed her mother out the front door.

Iris whispered to her sister, "You must have punched her hard!"

"I jabbed her like this," Martha Rose bunched up her fist and punched the air with a jerk. "She shoves little kids in the back and runs away. She shoved me today, and pushed me into a little boy, and he fell down. I chased her and boxed her in the stomick good."

Miss Davis knelt in front of Martha Rose. "Martha Rose Andersen, if you strike anyone in this school again, I will discipline you. I know it is hard to see a bully take advantage of people, but to hit Lily in the stomach is not acceptable. When Lily returns, I want you two to eat lunch together with me for a week." She rose to her full five feet and turned to Iris' mother. "One day I will tell you Mrs. Carlson's story." She looked at Iris and tilted her head. "Iris, how to you manage to get in the middle of things? And who is this handsome young man?" She stroked Ben's smooth head, and he burped.

"Trouble maker?"

On the way to her classroom Iris wondered about the name Carlson. If Lily had five brothers they must go to this school. She stopped walking. Why, Lars Carlson was in her class! He was younger than Iris but in the same grade. There was an Eliot Carlson in Merry's class. Both were tall and thin. Lars was stoop-shouldered and drew pictures all the time. Mrs. Nilsen let him take art books home from the classroom. Iris suspicioned that her teacher brought books from home. There was a mystery here. Iris would get to the bottom of it.

Iris kept her eye on Lars Carlson, his bony spine bent over his desk two rows in front of her. He kept a pencil behind his ear. At recess and lunch he sketched friends at play. One day Iris found herself an object of his intense study. She was swinging and had pumped and pumped until she glided high. She leaned back and looked at the sky. Each time she swooped to earth she saw Lars staring at her then at his sketch pad. She let the momentum of the swing slow to a stop, and sat there, her arms wrapped around the ropes. When Lars glanced up, he met her eyes. She got up, walked over to him, and glanced at the sketch. She drew in her breath. "Goodness gracious!" she gasped. "That's me!"

Lars laughed at her reaction and Iris was startled by his

deep rumbling voice. "Yes. It certainly is."

"I mean, that is me. That's how I feel when I swing." Iris sat on a bench near Lars who was sitting on the grass. "I had no idea anyone could draw that!"

Lars handed her the picture. "If it is you, then you should have it."

Iris looked at the sketch. On paper was the rush and thrill of reaching the highest peak of the swing. Trees were smudges in the sky and clouds were directly overhead. There she floated, her hair lifted by the wind, her arms straining to hold herself back to look at the sky.

Iris took the paper by the edges. "I had no idea," she repeated.

Lars' pale face began to pink under his hair which was as white and blonde as his mother's.

Iris changed the subject. "My little sister punched your little sister in the stomach. I'm sorry."

Lars ducked his head, and his hair fell over his eyes. "I know. You don't have to be sorry. My sister is a beast. She yells, shouts, and roars like . . . like . . ." He let his sentence fade. "She's not like other little girls."

Iris said, "My sister's a wild animal, too. One spring she got pecked in the face by our rooster, then she fell in the hay loft and cracked her head. We never know what Martha Rose will do next."

"Your sister isn't mean. Mine is," said Lars.

"Oh, my mother wouldn't let Martha Rose be mean. My daddy won't either. Does it help if your daddy speaks to her?"

"My father doesn't live with us," said Lars. He gathered his pad and jammed his pencil behind his ear. He stood up like a hero gathering his armor and said, "He's in a mental hospital. Now, go and tell everybody we're crazy!" He loped away with long angry strides.

Iris sat on the bench. She wanted to call after him. She was angry he'd jumped to the conclusion that she would tell everyone his father was crazy. Then she was sad he had given up and walked away. There was dignity to the way he stooped over his drawings. Iris wasn't finished with Lars, no sir-ree.

That afternoon she and Julie walked to Julie's house after school. Iris thought about Lars. He rode a red bike to school every day and left it on the ground next to younger children's bikes. After school he rode towards town. Today he cycled around the playground to avoid the girls.

"Isn't that Lars Carlson," Iris asked.

Julie smiled. "It is. What's on your mind, Iris Anderson?"

"You remember when Martha Rose socked his sister in the stomach? I wonder where he lives. I saw his mother when she came to school. She's tiny and thin, like Lars, but about Merry's size." She gave her friend a steady look. "That's all."

Julie pointed to a row of shops the block beyond her family's Creamery. "He and his family live over the hardware store. They go the Catholic church. His mother's a seamstress. Tell me why you want to know."

Iris opened her notebook and took out the pencil sketch Lars had done. "Look at this," she said.

"Oh, oh!" Julie stood on the sidewalk and stared at the drawing. "Let's show this to my mother." The girls hurried into Julie's house.

Julie stamped up the steps, burst into the living room, and ran to the kitchen to find her mother. Mrs. Gonner welcomed the girl's entrance with a happy, "Hello!"

"Mother, look!" Julie was breathless as she held the sketch out for her mother.

Mrs. Gonner sat down in a kitchen chair with the picture in front of her. "He gets better all the time. I've seen Lars' sketches on the bulletin board when I visit the school. This one is special." She handed the picture to Iris. "Sit down. I'll get cookies and milk."

Iris could hardly wait until the three of them settled in the kitchen. The girls chose warm cookies from the platter in front of them. Iris took two oatmeal cookies plump with raisins and nuts. "You do make the best cookies, Mrs. Gonner. Tell us about the Carlsons."

Mrs. Gonner's face took on a serious expression. "Iris, some people aren't as lucky as others. Mrs. Carlson, Annie's her name, has a hard life. Her husband, Gunther Carlson, was a famous painter, studied in France, won prizes for his water colors, had shows in New York, Chicago, you name it. A year ago he had a mental breakdown. The family lived in Norway at the time. Gunther was born there. Annie made a tough decision. She and the family returned to Minnesota, where she was born. Mr. Carlson is in an institution in Wisconsin. Annie came to Harmony because it's small and not far from her husband. That woman has five sweet boys, every one of them, and that spiteful little girl. The boys have jobs after school and help as much as they can. Lars is as talented as his father. When I see light burning in their apartment late into the night, I know Annie is sewing, or mending. It is the only income they have, except for what the boys bring home.

Iris stopped eating. "Why doesn't someone do something?"

Mrs. Gonner smiled, this time, a sad smile, "What could anyone do? The church members at St. Gabriel's are wonderful but you must be careful not to do too much. Feelings get hurt. It's often hard to know what's the best thing to do."

Iris stood and picked the picture up off the table. "I have to go. Thank you for the great cookies."

"Iris, you just got here," complained Julie.

"I have to talk to mother. She'll know what to do." Before her friends could protest, she was gone.

When Iris saw her mother and Ben in the yard, she broke into a run. Her mother was surprised to see her and said, "I thought you were going to spend the afternoon with Julie."

"I was," said Iris gulping to catch her breath. "Mother, we have to do something about the Carlsons. I had to come home and tell you because you always know what to do!"

"The Carlsons?" Laura Ellen looked puzzled.

"Oh, Mother!" Iris' voice pleaded with her mother to understand.

"You mean Lily's mother," said Laura Ellen. "What's wrong?"

"Everything!" Iris was near tears. "We have to help."

Iris' mother looked at her daughter's ernest face and shifted Ben to her other hip. "Let's go inside."

Iris told her mother what she'd heard about Lars and his family. She pulled the drawing out of her school book and her mother studied it. She put her hands flat on the kitchen table. "You're right. Lars is a real artist. He'll succeed even if we don't do anything. This talent will be recognized. What a gift he has." She folded her hands in her lap and stared at the ceiling. "What we need to do is help that woman, and child. Lily's had a confusing life. No wonder she's rowdy. Imagine growing up in foreign country, her father loses his mind, and they come to a strange country and town, where her mother works all day."

Iris said, "When we moved to Minnesota I felt like I'd come to a foreign country! I know how they feel. Lars has a Norwegian accent, but my southern accent makes people stare more. What can we do for them, Mother?"

"People here are used to Scandinavian accents, but not southern ones. I think I need to have a few dresses altered. I'll never have the waist I had before you babies came. I'll visit Annie Carlson."

Iris smiled as her mother began to nod her head and plan. That night Iris heard the murmur of her mother and father's voices late into the night. She knew the two of them would do all they could to make life better for the Carlson family.

When Iris, Merry, and Martha Rose came home from school the next day, they saw a bicycle at the back door, and heard laughter before they got inside. Annie Carlson and Laura Ellen sat at the kitchen table, eating pound cake with rhubarb sauce. When the girls came in, Mrs. Carlson jumped up. "Oh! Time got away from me. I must hurry home to be there when Lily arrives."

"I'll come next week for my dresses," called Laura Ellen.

Annie Carlson cycled down the drive with two dresses under her arm.

Laura Ellen looked at Iris and said, "I have a new friend."

While the girls were in school, Laura Ellen and Annie Carlson visited once a week. Iris was impressed as her mother's persistent presence began to make a difference in the way Mrs. Carlson began to appear. Her face was fuller, and there was a hint of pink in her cheeks. Iris' mother would say she had done too much baking, then she'd take a loaf of bread or bag of cookies when she visited the seamstress' shop over the hardware store. She told Iris she couldn't wait for the day she would take her to see "the most interesting apartment in Harmony, Minnesota. Maybe in all of Minnesota."

The following Saturday Iris got her chance. Her mother canned the last of the late tomatoes, and decided to take four jars of the jewel-red vegetables to town and drop them at the Carlson's while Horace went into the hardware store. Iris carried Benjamin up a dark stairway. The door at the top of the stairs opened, and a shaft of sunlight brightened the way. Ben squirmed in her arms. Her mother laughed. "Ben loves to come here."

When Iris walked into the apartment, she knew why. There was color everywhere. Paintings of flowers and children covered the walls of the tiny living space. Vases of fall flowers and bright branches of leaves were on every surface. Bolts of fabric were stacked on a bookcase like a work of art. Annie Carlson, pale and blonde in the midst of that intense color was an oasis. Iris had never seen walls the color of this apartment. They were red. No one in Harmony painted anything red! Well, a barn, maybe. Mrs. Carlson smiled at Ben and leaned forward to take him from Iris. Ben waved his arms and reached for his new friend. Iris' mother said, "What do you think?"

Iris wandered from painting to painting. In the lower right hand corner of each one in a tiny script, was the name, 'Gunther Carlson.' She turned to Mrs. Carlson, "Do you have every one of your husband's paintings?"

Annie laughed, "Goodness, no. Gunther has pictures in

galleries in New York, Chicago, Stockholm, and London. Friends in Europe are storing some for us. These are the ones I couldn't part with. They are our family pictures."

Iris' mother said, "Walk down the hall. Annie's sewing room is there with a lot more pictures."

Iris walked down a hallway painted sky blue. The paintings here stood out against the color. The 'sewing' room was a tiny space, yellow, and the pictures were of blonde children. Iris knew which one was Lars. There was a day bed along one wall with an orange and green quilt on it. The bedside table held a Bible in Norwegian. This was where Annie Carlson worked and slept. Iris wondered where the children slept.

She came into the living room. "I have never been in such a beautiful place in my life."

"You're kind," said Mrs. Carlson, blushing. "When I have Gunther's paintings near me, he is close."

Laura Ellen said, "Iris is not being kind. She's being honest." She turned to her daughter, "Mr. Carlson is coming home for a visit this weekend. Isn't that the best news?"

Iris looked at the two women. Her mother's face was bright with excitement. She took Annie's hand in hers. "I'll bring some eggs on Friday. We have too many eggs, and our family is tired of custard. I hope you can use them."

Mrs. Carlson looked around the apartment. "I hope Gunther likes it here. If this visit works out, if Gunther feels settled, the doctor may consider letting him stay." Annie sat on a wooden chair with Benjamin in her lap. "He'll need a place to work," she added.

Iris' mother said, "Annie, take one day at a time. If you try to tackle all your problems at once, they'll overwhelm you. Your husband will find a place to paint." She hoisted Ben onto her right hip, and looked at him. "I'll be so glad when you learn to walk."

"Be careful what you wish for," said Mrs. Carlson.

Iris thought of Gunther Carlson all week. In her mind, she

imagined him in the bright apartment. Lars stayed bent over his desk, and sketched at every recess. He was drawing the young classes now, Martha Rose's group.

The following Saturday, Iris begged to go to town with her father. He needed a handle for his axe. He parked the car in front of the hardware store and Iris looked up at the windows of the Carlson apartment. There was not a soul in sight. Her father weighed and stroked every handle in the store. Iris gave up on him, and wandered around. She went outside to sit on the wide steps. The sky was cloudless, her favorite shade of autumn blue. She put her chin in her hands. The door to the Carlson's apartment opened and out stepped a tall white-haired man. He had an easel under one arm and a flat wooden box under the other. He continued down the steps and into the street without a glance at her. Iris grinned. He walked like Lars, a loping stride that carried him out of sight.

As her father drove home, Iris kept a look-out for Mr. Carlson. Before they turned off the main road, she saw him in a field. He'd set up his easel and stood in front of it. When their car passed he made one long stroke of blue at the top of the blank canvas.

At that moment, Iris knew in her heart the Carlsons were together. The artist had found a place to work. Harmony would be proud to have him.

Chapter Two

OCTOBER

Two weeks into the month of October Iris accompanied her father to town again. She wanted to get out of the house. Specks of snow danced off the windshield. Iris huddled in her coat. Her father had a list of errands. He needed to make a delivery of pies to church for the evening's Harvest Dinner. They would take a jar of vegetable soup to Dr. Brenna who had a nasty cold. Iris' mother assured the doctor that her soup was the best medicine in town, after his, of course. Final stop, the hardware store. Horace needed nails and excuse to sit by the central stove and swap news with other farmers who were in town for 'nails.'

When Iris entered the store, the smell of leather, steel and oil met her, then her eye was caught by a spot of color over the cash register. At first all she saw was yellow, but as she and her father joined the small group in front of the counter, she recognized a wheat field, and the work of Mr. Carlson. Iris could feel the breeze that bent the bright grain.

Several farmers stood staring. Iris listened to their comments.

"Pure genius, that's what I say."

"Makes our wheat fields down-right holy."

"Don't see how he paints in that wind!"

A well-dressed gentleman Iris hadn't seen in Harmony spoke up, "Is it for sale?"

Mr. Crocker, the hardware store owner, stood behind the counter. "No sir! Not this one. This is a gift. It's not going anywhere. Anybody who wants to look can stay as long as they like."

The newcomer asked, "Can you tell me where to find Mr. Carlson?"

Iris thought, Ah-ha! He knows Gunther Carlson!

Mr. Crocker asked, "Who's looking for him?"

"My name is Charles Betts." He held his hand across the counter to shake Mr. Crocker's. "How do you do. I wasn't looking for Mr. Carlson when I came in. I wanted directions. Now, I can't take my eyes off this landscape. I knew it was Gunther's. I'd like to speak to him if I could. Does he live in town?"

"You know Mr. Carlson," asked Mr. Crocker.

Mr. Betts held out his hands and looked at them. "I studied with Gunther in France for a year. I came back to the states and finished an Art History degree at the University of Minnesota. Now I'm head of the Fine Arts department at St. Sebastian College. I'd appreciate knowing how to get in touch with Gunther."

The door to the store opened, and Annie Carlson entered. She took in the scene at the cash register. Mr. Betts saw her and broke away from his conversation. He walked towards Mrs. Carlson with arms outstretched.

Annie stepped back until recognition dawned on her face. Iris thought her smile looked like the sun coming out. Mrs. Carlson fell into the tall man's embrace and began to cry. "I feel like I'm looking at a ghost," she said. Then she wiped her teary face. "Charles Betts! After all this time. What brings you to Harmony Minnesota?" She began to laugh. "Come upstairs. Seeing you will make Gunther happy."

Mr. Betts hesitated. "I don't want to upset him. I heard . . ." he let the sentence drop.

"You heard he was in a mental institution," said Mrs. Carlson.

"I did. It made me sad. I see he's painting again," Mr. Betts smiled. "I tried to buy this . . . ."

"Follow me," Mrs. Carlson said, leading the way out the door.

Iris was tempted to tag along. She wanted to see the reunion. Instead, she watched as Mrs. Carlson hooked her arm in Charles Betts' arm and begin to chatter as they passed the plate glass window on their way upstairs to the apartment.

The following Wednesday morning Iris walked up the broad school steps and saw Lars standing just inside the door. He appeared to be waiting. When Iris opened the big door, he stepped forward. "We're leaving," was all he said, and began to walk away.

Iris grabbed his shirt sleeve. "Wait! Who's leaving? You can't come up to someone and say, 'we're leaving' and walk away!"

Lars stood silently. Iris thought how much he was like his father, both men of few words. She said, "You are your father are 'two peas in a pod.'

Lars' eyebrows raised so high they disappeared under his fringe of hair.

"Tell me," said Iris.

"My family is moving to St. Sebastian. There is a small college, and my father has a job to teach art." He looked shyly happy. "This is good luck. My family isn't used to it."

Iris was shocked. Her mother would be too. She would miss Annie Carlson, her new friend.

"We're not leaving until December," Lars continued. My father's working on a painting he says he can't put off. Mother told us this morning. I wanted you to know first." He finally smiled. It was the first true smile Iris had seen from this lanky boy. His mouth spread into a wide grin. "He's doing a Nativity painting for the Catholic church. No one's seen it. He's not usually this secretive."

The school bell rang and both of them jumped. Iris laughed. "Well, that woke me up! Tell Mrs. Nilsen right away. She'll be happy for your family."

Iris could hardly wait to get home and share the news with her mother. Mr. Carlson has a job! She ran the last few yards to her back door.

Her mother was scraping applesauce off Benjamin's

cheeks. She looked up as Iris ran into the house. Iris blurted out, "I've got news!"

"Why, so do I," said her mother. "I've got good news."

Iris' face fell. "About the Carlsons?" she asked.

"Yes. How do you know?"

"I wanted to be the first to tell you. Lars told me this morning." She grinned at her mother, "Isn't it great! Mr. Carlson has a job."

Her mother added, "They'll have a house to themselves, faculty housing, it's called. Gunther will have a studio at the college where he can paint. They cycled over this morning. I've never seen Annie happy like this."

"Yes," said Iris, "a good beginning."

"Before Gunther leaves, he wants to do a Nativity painting for the Catholic church. He wants to give something to people who cared for his family and for him. He rarely speaks, but if you're quiet, he will talk. Benjamin sat on his lap and pulled his beard this morning, and that man sat there and laughed and laughed! I thought Annie would burst with excitement."

Iris asked, "Where is St. Sebastian?"

"Only sixty miles away. Annie and I plan to visit each other. Miles can't separate us. She's the sister I never had."

That evening Laughing Sky, Uncle Luke, and baby Anna walked across the pasture to have dinner with the Andersens. They would celebrate Iris' fifteenth birthday. In the spring, the couple and their adopted Ojibway daughter would begin work on a house behind the Andersen's barn. Right now Laughing Sky's cabin, a meadow away for Iris' family farm house, overflowed with bookcases, her loom, a small bed downstairs for Anna, and a dining room table and four chairs from Luke's house in Bemidji. Uncle Luke hadn't started looking for a job. He and Laughing Sky had been married four months.

Luke brought a loaf of Swedish Rye for the dinner. Anna had begun to walk that week. Iris followed the wobbly child around the house. Anna grabbed for every support she could find. Her chubby fist found the tail end of the table cloth, and she pulled hard. Luke reached for the pitcher of milk on the corner of the table and Horace grabbed the sugar bowl. Anna tottered and sat down hard. Iris let out a sigh of relief. "What in the world will we do when Ben starts to walk," she wondered out loud.

Iris' mother had made the family's favorite dessert, spice cake with raisins.

Uncle Luke asked Martha Rose, "What happened to the little girl you punched this fall?"

"She's my friend!"

Iris's mother told her brother-in-law, "That was Lily Carlson, Gunther's daughter."

Uncle Luke looked surprised. "That is the kindest man I've ever met. I see him in town, or painting on the side of the road. Snow doesn't stop him. Wind doesn't stop him. Don't tell me they have a hell cat of a little girl!"

Iris' mother raised her eyebrows, "Lily has had a difficult young life. She is much improved now that her father is home, and Dr. Brenna found that after several severe ear infections, she has a hearing loss."

Uncle Luke looked thoughtful, "I have some news," he said.

Iris and her mother laughed. "We already know," said Iris. "The Carlson's are moving to St. Sebastian."

"They are?" he said.

Iris asked, "So, Uncle Luke, what's your news?"

He began, "Gunther is going to illustrate my new book of poetry. We met yesterday for me to read to him. I wish you could have seen his eyes. I rarely meet people who are so happy to listen. He began to sketch as I read, and with a few strokes, made the page come alive. I'm honored he wants to contribute his sketches to my book."

Laughing Sky laid her hand on her husband's arm, "Luke, Gunther said he was honored also."

Merry asked, "What are these poems about, Uncle Luke?"

He took a deep breath and exhaled. "I decided to take some good and advice and write what I know. My poems are centered in Harmony. The pictures are a secret. I promised Gunther I wouldn't tell his plans."

Horace asked his brother, "Do you have a publisher?"

Luke grinned, "Always the practical one! Yes, I have a publisher. They sputtered with joy when I told them Gunther Carlson wants to illustrate the book. It will come out in the spring."

"What's the name of the book," asked Iris.

"Poems from Harmony," her uncle replied. "I'll sign a copy for you." He looked at her, tilted his head and asked, "What happened to your face?"

Iris put her hands to her face and felt for a scratch or blemish. "What do you mean?" She turned to her mother, "What's the matter with my face," she asked.

Her uncle smiled. "There's nothing wrong with your face. You've changed. You used to look like a little girl, and now, well, look at you! Iris, you are one beautiful young woman!"

Iris felt her face turn red. She grinned at her uncle and crossed her eyes. "Stop looking at me!"

Her uncle continued to examine her face.

"Stop looking at me!" she ordered.

Uncle Luke said, "I couldn't wait until we open presents. Iris, here's your gift." Iris unwrapped a framed mirror. It was square, about a foot wide, two feet tall, and the frame was painted white, pure white. Uncle Luke said, "I want you to be able to see yourself. It's important. I'm trying to figure out who you look like. You certainly have the Andersen hair and eyes, all blonde, blue and Norwegian, but something's different. You look like . . . yourself."

Iris could tell that her mother was pre-occupied with thoughts of the Carlson's move. She'd find her standing in front of the linen closet with a stack of towels in her arms, immobile, staring. Then she'd shake her head and continue her task. Iris' mother spent a lot of time going through Merry's out-grown clothes. Merry turned eleven, and her father said his middle girl was shooting up like an asparagus. Her mother made a pile of clothes for Martha Rose, and a pile for Lily. Martha Rose said she didn't want to wear her sister's clothes. 'After all,' she said, 'my name is not Merry!'

There was a calmness in Iris' mother that was new. The fact was, the whole family had relaxed this fall. Iris decided the Carlsons were the reason. They were a gift. Snow began in ernest in mid-October. Iris' mother often held Ben in her arms, swaying back and forth in front of the kitchen window pointing at the snow. Ben kicked, drooled, pointed, and said, "O! O!" It was a close to "snow" as he could manage.

Everybody knew what he meant. His dark eyes took on a shine. Iris saw skis in his future.

She hung the mirror from Uncle Luke and Laughing Sky next to the door of her room. Every time she left and walked into the hall, she caught sight of herself, her real self.

Chapter Three

NOVEMBER

Iris sat on her mother's bed and watched her unpin her wavy black hair and begin to brush it. "Mother, why don't Merry, Martha Rose, or I have hair like yours?"

"I don't know. I'm a mis-fit in this family of blondes."

"Daddy says Ben's hair's getting dark. It's funny that the boy in the family has curls and looks like you. The girls look like daddy. Do you think I look like you?"

Her mother studied her daughter's reflection in her dresser mirror. "I'd like to think we do. You're more beautiful every day."

"Oh, Mother," said Iris. She made a face in the mirror.

"When someone says you are beautiful, the reply is, 'Thank you.'"

Iris imitated her mother's voice, "Thank you. Uncle Luke embarrassed me the other night. Look at me." Iris stood up. "I'm flat as a barn board, pale as milk, and my hair hangs down like old string."

Her mother responded, "No. You are fair, supple, and you hair is a silk fringe."

Iris laughed. "You sound like a mother!"

Her mother asked, "What do you think about my hair?" She had brushed it until it lay around her shoulders in a dark mass.

"Your hair," Iris asked.

"My hair, for a change. Do you think I should wear it down like this? Should I stop wearing that bun on top of my head? Does it make me look old?"

Iris looked at her mother, "This is the first time in my life you have asked me anything like that. Something's going on."

Her mother said, "Is it obvious? Nothing upsetting is 'going on.' I do have a secret which will be shared soon. I promised to keep it to myself. It's a good secret."

"I knew it! I can always tell when I'm right. When will we find out," asked Iris.

"Before Christmas," her mother replied. She added, "I'm not pregnant."

Iris laughed, "Good!"

Early in November, Iris' mother invited Earl, and Oscar Runs Like Fox to Thanksgiving dinner. Uncle Luke, Laughing Sky, and Anna would come. One evening at the dinner table, Iris asked her mother if they could invite the Carlsons for Thanksgiving. "They'll leave soon, and I bet they don't have an invitation from anybody else. We could at least ask."

"You're thoughtful, Iris," said her mother. "I did ask Annie to bring her family. She said there would be too many people. I think the real reason is that Gunther's shy. Except for Lily, the whole family is shy."

"I wish they'd come," sighed Iris.

Martha Rose said, "There sure would be a lot of people!"

"If they came, we'd figure out where to put them. It would make Thanksgiving complete," said her mother.

Merry asked, "Are you going to make Grannie's corn pudding this year? You forgot last year."

"And smashed potato dressing," added Martha Rose.

"And sweet potato pie, pecan pie, sour cream raisin pie, and rocky road cake," added Iris.

"My stomach hurts thinking about it," said their father.

"Earl's going to bring rolls. He's taken an interest in bread making, like your Uncle Luke," said their mother. "I'm sure he misses his wife and the traditions they'd begun."

"Yes. Oscar, too. He must miss his mother something awful," said Iris.

"I wish I'd known her," said her mother. "Everyone says Ava was beautiful."

Iris spoke up, "She was."

Merry piped up, "And how do you know?"

Iris remembered waking from her dream last year and seeing a blonde woman sitting in her chair before she faded from view. "I know," she said. "Oscar told me what she looked like." That wasn't a lie. Oscar had told her the first year her family moved to Harmony. Her mother had gone to Richmond after Iris' grandfather died. Oscar had led Iris to the secret place where he and his mother had sat. Lady Slippers were in bloom.

"How big is the turkey," asked Martha Rose.

Her father held out his hands big enough to measure the size of Cookie, their farm dog. "This big!"

Martha Rose's eyes got big. "I can smell it already!"

A week before Thanksgiving Iris, Martha Rose, and Merry walked home from school. Snow crunched and their noses were red from the cold wind. Merry stopped and pointed. "Look!"

Iris followed the direction of her sister's gloved hand. In the middle of a snowy field stood Gunther Carlson. His head was muffled in a red scarf, and he was bundled in a big blue coat. He painted gloveless. He had painted this field so many times he looked like he belonged there. Most of the people of Harmony were used to seeing him there. He'd bought the haystack so he could paint it all year. Every painting was different.

Martha Rose took off running across the stubbled field. Iris called after her, "Martha Rose, don't bother Mr. Carlson!" She might as well have been yelling at the wind. She and Merry followed their little sister across the snow.

The artist never stopped staring at the scene in front of him. Today he had a sketch pad and charcoal stick. At present, the paper was blank. Martha Rose spoke up, "Would you please eat turkey with us on Thanksgiving?" She looked up at the artist, and the hood of her coat fell away. The wind sifted about her face, and her hair blew like corn silk.

Gunther Carlson looked down at the child and grunted,

"Huh!" He looked again at the snowy field.

Martha Rose reached over and tugged at his coat.

Iris said, "Leave Mr. Carlson alone. He's concentrating."

Martha Rose continued, "Mother says it would make her day," she said in a cheerful voice.

Mr. Carlson put his charcoal stick in his pocket. The girls watched as the red-wrapped head began a slow nod.

"Is that, yes," asked Martha Rose. "Say, yes."

A raspy under-used voice said, "Ja. Ve come."

He took Martha Rose by the shoulder and moved her in front of him. "Stay."

Mr. Carlson began to sketch the little girl. He tore the page from the pad and gave it to her. To Iris he called, "Ja. Ve come!"

Iris saw a twinkle in his eye. His serious mouth twitched in a tiny smile. He waved his arms. "Go! Go home! Too cold!"

The girls ran all the way home. Martha Rose held the sketch in front of her like a shield.

As soon as dawn began to lighten the room, Iris' eyes opened. She snuggled under her quilts and a shiver of excitement ran through her. Today Gunther Carlson was coming to her house for Thanksgiving dinner. She pushed aside the cats, Muffin and Biscuit. Why wouldn't they sleep with Martha Rose? They were her cats! She put on her slippers and robe, and ran down the stairs. Her mother and father were having their first cup of coffee. Iris kissed them, first a peck on her mother's cheek, then one on her father's forehead. Horace hugged his daughter, "How did you sleep," he asked.

"Too long!" answered Iris.

Her mother smiled, "Iris, it's seven o'clock. We have six hours until company arrives. Which is the object of your impatience, Oscar, or Lars?"

"Oh, Mother, all you think about is boys. Don't you realize that THE Gunther Carlson is coming to our house? He's a world famous artist! I'll never forget this day as long as I live. I can't wait to write Grandmother and Dorothy." She let out a big gust of breath, "Pshew!"

Her mother said, "He visits with Annie."

"That's not the same. He is going to come into my house, sit down, and eat with my family. Imagine!" Iris threw her hands in the air.

Her father said, "Iris, you are headed for the stage."

"I'm not eating breakfast," said Iris. "I don't have time. I'm going to wash my hair and get dressed. May I set the table?"

"Of course! That would be a big help. I am going to put a small table in the dining room for the little children."

"Oh, please don't make me sit with them," cried Iris.

"Don't worry. Uncle Luke and Laughing Sky have said they'd sit with the little ones. You won't have to sit with Martha Rose, Lily, Ben, or Annie."

Iris came downstairs with her hair wrapped in a towel. The fragrance of Watkin's Lemon Rinse hovered about her like a halo. She went to the heavy oak table and stood at one end, imagining how she would arrange the candles and dishes. She opened the chest that held table linens. The long yellow tablecloth that Earl Runs Like Fox had liked so much caught her eye. No. Today was a formal event. Yellow wouldn't do. There was her grandmother's lace cloth. Perfect. She tugged it free and laid it on the table. She called into the kitchen. "I need someone to help me put the leaves in the table."

Her father got up from his toast and rhubarb preserves. "I'll help."

Together the two of them lifted the wooden pieces into place, expanding the length of the table by several feet.

"Mother, do we have enough plates," asked Iris.

"Yes, just enough," her mother called back.

Iris returned to her work. She smoothed the ivory lace cloth in place, put two silver candle sticks on each side of the empty space reserved the the turkey platter. The candle sticks had been a wedding present for her parents from her mother's brother. Her mother saved two tall beeswax candles for today. Near the candle sticks Iris placed pine cones saved from a hike in the woods on top of yellow and red leaves, curling, but colorful. She looked at the kitchen clock and moaned, "Only nine o'clock." She heard her father stifle a laugh.

The clock moved in slow motion. The morning crawled. Iris kept an eye on the table to make sure Ben and Martha Rose stayed away from it. Ben was in his lively mood, sensing the importance of the day. The smell of turkey baking made Iris' mouth water, and she helped her mother by washing pot after pot, and putting breakfast dishes away. Still the hours crept. Iris had chosen a lilac dress that had been her mother's. She like the way the skirt swirled around her legs. She brushed and brushed her shoulder-length blonde hair, and held it back from her face with a deep purple ribbon.

Martha Rose was in the middle of her bed playing with three naked dolls. "I have to dress my children," she declared.

"Hurry up! I'll find something for you to wear." She began to look through her sister's closet. She chose a white blouse with a wide collar, and a soft blue corduroy skirt.

Martha Rose took one look and said, "I love that skirt. I'll wear my hat!"

"Martha Rose, you don't need a hat for dinner."

"I always wear a hat with that skirt. Mrs. Ludvigson wears a hat," she insisted.

Iris put her hands on her hips and glared at her sister.

"You look like mother when you do that," Martha Rose said with a grin.

"You can dress yourself. I give up." Iris stalked down the stairs.

Her father had his coat on ready to drive to town and pick up the Carlsons. "I don't know where they'll all sit," he wondered aloud.

Laughing Sky and Luke came in the door as Iris' father left to pick up the Carlsons. Anna reached out her arms for Iris, and hugged her neck in a tight embrace. "You're going to choke me," exclaimed Iris. She took Anna in her arms, and stood her on the floor. "I'll take your coat off. Oh, Anna, you look beautiful!" Anna had on a red plaid flannel dress that Laughing Sky had made. The child's coffee-colored cheeks were dusty pink from the cold walk across the pasture. When Iris took her hat off, electricity made the baby's fine hair stand up like black silk.

There was a honk of a horn outside. Iris looked out the kitchen window and saw Earl and Oscar getting out of their pick-up truck. Each of them carried a basket.

By the time they'd hung their coats on the rack at the back door, Iris heard her father's car. Time began to race. After the long wait for one o'clock to arrive, Iris wanted time to stand still again. The back door opened and eight Carlsons trooped in. Lily and Merry took Anna and Ben and began to play with them like they were dolls. Iris' father tried to make introductions, but was jostled and patted on the back. Mr. Carlson handed her father his black hat and his blue coat. Iris thought he looked like a preacher. He had on a white shirt starched stiff, and a black bow-tie. He had a fined quilted vest on over his shirt. It was embroidered with twining vines. She had never seen such a beautiful vest on a man before. They heard a voice on the stairs and Martha Rose came into the room. Iris's shoulders sagged as she thought, oh, not today! Her little sister trailed a gauzy veil from a wide-brimmed sun hat. She looked for Earl Runs Like Fox and sang, "You Are My Sunshine." Her voice rang through the kitchen. Conversation stopped as Martha Rose stood in front of her friend, looked up from under her hat and finished with, "please don't take my sunshine away."

Iris was appalled at her sister hogging attention, but to her surprise, every one clapped. Really, thought Iris, little kids can get away with anything.

Earl stooped down and greeted Martha Rose. Mr. Carlson knelt before her, took her hand and kissed it. Iris rolled her eyes.

In the quiet, her father announced, "This kitchen is the busiest place in our house and today is no exception. Let's spread out a bit so the food can make its way to the table."

Martha Rose kept Gunther's hand in hers and led him to the living room. "You'll sit with me," she commanded. The tall man smiled down at her. Iris's heart fell. She wouldn't get a chance to be with this great man after all. He was going to sit at the children's table!

When the guests had gathered at their chairs in the living room and the dining room, the guests stood and held hands, making a huge circle. Horace said, "In honor of our heritage, and our guests, let's say the blessing in Norwegian." All voices joined together.

I Jesu namn till bords vi ga
valsigna Gud den mat vi fa. Amen

Next the clink of glasses, forks, knives, and laughing conversations began. Nothing turned out the way Iris planned. Earl and Gunther sat with the little children in the living room. Luke sat on one side of Iris, and Oscar on the other. She tried to listen to the talk at her table, but all she could hear was the deep rumble of Gunther's laugh, and Earl Runs Like Fox's occasional, "Ha!" Laughing Sky and Mark, the oldest Carlson son, sat across the table from her. Mark was sixteen, like Oscar. They went to the high school together. Iris had never met him. The meal droned on. Most of Iris' food remained uneaten on her plate.

The sound of her mother's voice brought her back to the present. "Would you and Mark help clear the table and take orders for desert?"

Iris jumped up and began to take dinner plates into the kitchen. She walked into the living room where the children were eating. Martha Rose sat in Gunther Carlson's lap. He had on her silly sun hat. His bow tie was crooked. Earl pulled out his harmonica from his pocket and began to play, 'In Your Easter Bonnet, with All the Frills Upon It.' Iris couldn't help herself. She burst into laughter.

Mark had followed her into the room, and he began to laugh also. He hugged Iris' shoulders, and said, "I haven't seen my father have this much fun in years. To hear him laugh is a miracle."

Iris looked up at him. He was taller than her father, and thin like his brother, Lars. His eyes were deep blue, and his smile made them squinch up and almost disappear. He was looking at her. His arm was still around her shoulder.

He asked, "Why haven't I met you? You're the girl Lars sketches. Now I know why." He grinned at her. Iris felt her grin widen to match his.

While Iris, Mark, Oscar, Laughing Sky, and Mrs. Carlson cleared the tables, Iris heard snatches of laughter and music from the living room. Horace and Uncle Luke brought in firewood for the fireplace. With many hands helping, the kitchen was soon neat and clean. Iris hurried into the living room to join the fun. Oscar's father played his harmonica, Gunther squeezed a make believe concertina, and hummed. Children tumbled on the carpet like puppies. Ben crawled up in Oscar's lap and patted his face, singing, "Ba-ba-ba-ba." Iris gave up on finding a chair, and settled next to the wall across from Gunther and Martha Rose. Oscar sat cross legged on one side of her, and Mark slid down the wall and sat next to her on the other side. He pulled his knees up to his chest and wrapped his arms around them.

Gunther stopped singing and pointed at Iris. Her heart almost quit beating. "See!" he exclaimed. Then he turned to his wife and said with his raspy voice, "Did I tell you? Ah!" He turned his smile on Iris and she thought the earth had stopped spinning.

The Carlsons were beautiful together. Except for Mark, all the boys, Lars, John, twins Matthew and Luke, and young Lily sat around him or leaned on him. They were all blonde like their mother.

The cozy fire crackled and sent blue flames and sparks up

the chimney. Ben crawled over to Lars and fell asleep in the boy's lap. Lars rubbed his fingers in Ben's curly dark hair.

Iris sat and listened to the conversations around her. Her mother and Mrs. Carlson offered advice on parenting to Laughing Sky, from sleeping schedules to breaking bad habits. Anna hooked her fingers in Laughing Sky's mouth every time the young woman picked her up. Iris listened with Lily and Martha Rose while Earl told them stories. Martha Rose was rarely this still. Uncle Luke and her father talked about the University of Minnesota. Oscar and Mark listened carefully. Iris' mother got up and turned on a lamp. A general quiet fell over the group. Gunther and his wife exchanged smiles. Annie nodded to him, and stood up. Iris thought, Oh, don't let them go so soon! She had hadn't had a conversation with Gunther Carlson yet.

Mark leaned over to her and said, "Here it comes!"

Lars sat up straight.

Mark said, "Just wait!"

"Are you leaving," Iris asked. "I never had a chance to talk to your father."

"My father doesn't 'talk.' He isn't comfortable with English. It takes him a long time to put words together, but it is not because he doesn't have anything to say. He's talked more today than I've heard since he got back." Mark smiled. "Oh, here's mother."

Mrs. Carlson came into the room carrying a large frame covered with a blanket. She sat it in a chair. Mr. Carlson shifted Martha Rose off of his lap, stood up, and took the frame from his wife. He turned to his gathered friends and said, "For Catholic church. I make painting." He removed the cover and held up a painting of The Madonna and Child. A hush fell and the room became so quiet that the clock seemed to boom in the house.

In the picture, Iris' mother sat on the floor of a hay-strewn stable wrapped in a rough dark blanket with Ben in her arms. The baby was caught in the motion of patting his mother's face.

In the picture, her mother's dark hair fell around her shoulders, and curly wisps escaped and framed her eyes. Her mother looked straight out from the painting. Gunther Carlson had frozen her mother and brother in time. This was her mother's secret. Light seemed to come from the painting. If Iris turned out the lamp, she felt they would still be able to see her mother and Ben. Iris crept close to the painting, awed by her mother's eyes and Ben's silky skin. Iris had seen this look on her mother's face before. She had seen it the night they drove away from the hospital after her father had fallen in the cave. She'd seen it the day her grandmother called to tell them that Iris' grandfather had died. This Madonna was a sad one. Iris' throat began to hurt, and she left the room. She walked through the kitchen straight out the back door to the barn. Joshua stood in his stall with a blanket over him. He looked at her as if to say, "Would you like to talk?"

The barn door creaked, and a voice asked, "Are you in here?"

It was Mark. Iris' heart skipped a beat. She swallowed and answered, "Here, in the first stall."

She saw the top of Mark's blonde head in the gloomy aisle of the barn. His hair caught the last of the light. "Your mother told me this is where you escape. Why did you leave?"

Iris didn't answer. She remembered her mother's eyes in the painting. Then she said, "It isn't right for mother to look sad forever. She's frozen like that. People will see it, - -" She couldn't finish.

"Look at the painting again," said Mark. "That impression was your first impression. The painting, and your mother, deserve more. Perhaps Mary and the baby Jesus do, too."

"What did I miss," Iris asked.

"You have to keep looking. It won't work if I tell you. This is art. You have to spend time 'long-looking.' I don't draw like my father or Lars, but I can see their paintings because I know how to look. I hope to own a gallery and sell their work someday. Next fall I go to the University of Minnesota to begin a degree in Art History."

Oscar called from the barn door. "Mark, Iris, come out here!"

Iris smiled at Oscar's voice. She wished he'd come into the barn. She wanted to ask him about the painting.

Mark and Iris walked out the barn doors. Everyone had their coats on and stared at the sky. Iris looked up. She gasped, "Ahhh!"

The sky danced with light, pale green folded in on pink. Pastels of every hue floated and flashed like colored lightning. She found Oscar, and he linked his arm in hers. "The Northern Lights," he explained.

Iris had heard of the Northern Lights, but nothing prepared her for a scene like this. Julie had told her about them. Uncle Luke had told her about them.. Mrs. Nilsen had talked about astronomy and told the class about the Northern Lights. Her third winter in Harmony held more than she could have expected.

Gunther Carlson's mouth was open in awe. "Not since Norge, Not since Norge."

His wife stood next to him, and he put his arms around her and held her tight. "Light! You!" he said.

Martha Rose took Earl's hand and said in a whispery voice, "Is it magic?"

Earl, who barely spoke more than Gunther Carlson answered, "Better than magic."

Chapter Four

DECEMBER

The temperature was fifteen degrees the day the Carlsons moved. A foot of snow fell the week before and lay hard and crunchy on the ground. Iris' mother packed a thermos of coffee and cinnamon rolls to take to the apartment on the morning of the big day. Her father planned to drive a covered truck that belonged to Mr. Crocker. Earl Runs Like Fox would drive his pickup truck. Iris' mother would drive the Carlson children. There was no room for the Andersen children, but Merry, Martha Rose, and Iris begged to accompany their mother to town to say good bye. The three girls would walk the mile home. Laughing Sky would stay at the house with Benjamin and Anna until Iris' parents returned.

When the Andersens arrived at the front door of the hardware store, Earl's truck and the van were parked in front. Gunther stood outside waving his arms, directing friends how to pack his blanket-wrapped paintings. Most of Harmony stood on the opposite sidewalk and watched as Mark, Earl, Oscar, and Uncle Luke came down the stairs with paintings under their arms. Iris' father ran up the apartment steps to help.

Mr. Crocker had hung a hand-lettered sign in the big window of the hardware store. It read, 'Best wishes to the Carlson family!'

Iris remembered her family's move from Virginia to Harmony two and a half years ago. Today she felt she'd always been here. Iris and her sisters went into the store to get warm. Mr. Crocker smiled and shook hands; Mrs. Crocker kept an enamel pot of coffee ready for the people helping with the move. Iris watched through the windows as her father and Mr. Carlson carried a dresser out; then Lars and Oscar followed with two bedside tables. Iris went out and asked if there was anything she could do.

"Sure, come on up," Lars called. "You might as well, the rest of the town is there already!"

The 'event' went on all morning. Many people crowded into the Carlson apartment but they jostled one another with good humor. Too quickly for Iris, the apartment was empty. Mrs. Carlson and Iris' mother spent most of the morning cleaning after the furniture was moved. They dusted the spot where the heavy trunk that held linens had stood and cleaned the kitchen and bathroom. When they finished, Mrs. Carlson took off her apron, folded it, and put it in her coat pocket. She hugged Laura Ellen hard. "This is not good bye," she declared.

Iris looked at the red wall, the yellow wall, and the bright blue hallway. She placed one palm against the living room wall. Out loud she said, "Good bye." This was good bye.

When Iris came of the door into the cold, clouds had formed in the West. Mark, Gunther, and her father were squeezed into the cab of the van, her father behind the wheel. Earl, Oscar and Lars were in the pickup truck. Laura Ellen shepherded the other children into the Andersen car. Mrs. Carlson hugged the Crockers, and the priest from the Catholic Church, Father Leo. Lars looked her way. He rolled the window down and leaned out. "Write me a letter!"

"I will! I will!" she called out.

Oscar leaned in front of Lars. "Hey, Iris, remember me? I'm coming back!"

The whole town of Harmony looked at Iris and smiled.

Mrs. Carlson squeezed into the front seat of the Andersen car. Lily was on her lap.

The van moved away, then the pick-up truck and car followed. Before the van turned the corner, the vehicle stopped. The passenger door opened and Gunther Carlson stepped out. He stood in the middle of the street, took off his hat, held it over his heart, and took a slow bow. Then he got into the van and vanished from the crowd's sight. A loud "Hurrah! went up from the community gathered on the hardware store porch. Iris swept tears from her cold cheeks. Mrs. Crocker circled her shoulders with an arm. "It was wonderful to know them," she said with a sigh.

Pastor and Mrs. Nilsen walked over to Iris. "We'll give you girls a ride home. You don't need to walk on this cold day." She looked at the sky. "Those clouds hold snow."

As the pastor's car moved away from the curb, Iris spoke up, "I feel like a balloon somebody let the air out of."

Merry added, "Christmas is coming and I don't even care."

Pastor Nilsen asked, "Martha Rose, don't you have anything to add?"

The little girl said, "I'm out of words."

The week before school was out, Martha Rose made an announcement. "Everybody listen to me. You are looking at a Christmas angel right now! I am going to be in the school pageant, with wings."

Her father raised an eyebrow, "An angel?"

Her mother grabbed Martha Rose and hugged her. "You'll make a perfect angel," she said.

"My class is the choir, and I have a solo," added Merry.

Her father asked, "Iris, what is the ninth grade going to do?"

"We're readers. I get to read the last part by myself."

Her mother smiled at the three girls, "I can hardly wait!"

"I need a big dress with sleeves that go down in points," said Martha Rose. Mrs. Nilsen is going to make wings and halos."

"That's good. We're fresh out of halos here," her father said.

Iris and Merry snickered, but Martha Rose turned up her nose. "Daddy, I am going to kneel by the manger with my arms crossed," she made an X with her arms over her chest, "until the curtain closes."

"We are so proud of you, Martha Rose," said her mother.

Iris spoke up. "Julie is going to be Mary. Mrs. Nielsen says that with her dark hair and eyes, she's perfect."

Iris spent days trying on dresses and skirts, even some of her mother's. She wanted just the right look for the pageant. Nothing suited her. With all her heart she wanted a red dress for Christmas. Mrs. Nilsen encouraged the readers to 'wear your best Sunday clothes.' Julie didn't have to worry. She'd be draped in a white sheet around her head, and a blue robe under it. She'd unbraid her hair, and let it hang below her shoulders.

Two days before the pageant, Iris walked into the kitchen with her Bible in her hands reading, "and there were in the same country shepherds abiding in the field keeping watch . . ." she looked up as her mother came in the door with a large box in her gloved hands. Her face was pink from the cold, but excitement lit her eyes. She put the package on the kitchen table and took off her gloves. "It's for you," she said.

Iris put her Bible on the table. "For me? It's not Christmas. Look, it's from Grandmother." She began to untie the strings. "Maybe I shouldn't open it yet," she said.

"Oh, you should," said her mother. "It is your Christmas gift but you are supposed to open it now."

Iris got the top off and pulled the tissue paper away. She drew in her breath and lifted out a red satin dress. Her fingers shook. "Mother! It has a lace collar! Look, no sash, only these tiny buttons! Oh, I have to try it on!"

"I can't wait to see you in it," said her mother.

"How did grandmother know?" Iris asked.

Her mother said, "Oh, you know grandmothers."

Iris looked at her. "You told her!" She smiled and hugged her mother. She and her mother were the same height. "Oh, I hope it fits."

Her mother lifted the dress over her daughter's head, and Iris turned her back to her mother to have the buttons done. "Listen to it, Mother." She swished the skirt around her legs.

"That is a lovely sound," agreed her mother. "It couldn't fit you better if you had tried it on for your grandmother."

"You mean, she made this," asked Iris.

"She did. I told her you were going to read in the pageant, and she said she'd make you a surprise."

"Did you tell her I wanted a red dress," asked Iris.

"I didn't know you wanted a red dress," said her mother. "Look at yourself."

Iris looked into her mother's vanity mirror. Her hands went to her cheeks. "Oh my, Oh my," was all she could say.

The dress fit her slender body to perfection. It dipped in the front where it joined a full skirt with a deep hem. The only decoration was the white lace collar.

The next day Iris' class stayed for the final dress rehearsal of the pageant. The shepherds wore bathrobes with cloths draped over their heads tied in place with rope. They carried long poles, and one boy had a lantern that would be lit for the play.

Iris watched as Julie's mother pinned a blue cloth on her daughter's head. Mrs. Gonner was in charge of costumes. Iris spoke up, "Julie, you look like you could be my mother's daughter. You are both dark and small. Sometimes I wish I could be tiny like you are. I'm already tall as mother. Who do you look like?"

Julie and her mother exchanged glances. Mrs. Gonner finished draping a fold in her daughter's shawl, sat down and hugged her girl. "Tell your friend," she said.

Iris drew back in the squeaky auditorium seat. "Tell me what?"

Julie pulled her lips together in a straight line, and announced, "I was adopted when I was three days old. My mother was Jewish. That is all I know about my real family. Mother and Daddy went to St. Paul to get me and bring me home."

Mrs. Gonner added, "Yes, in a snow storm! This little darling slept all the way."

She wiped her eyes. "It was Christmas Eve."

"No wonder you're a perfect Mary," said Iris.

"Attention!" Mrs. Nilsen clapped her hands. "Let's begin."

Iris followed Julie to the backstage area. She whispered to her friend, "I knew you were special."

Iris couldn't keep her mind on school work. She watched the low clouds and worried that snow would cancel the pageant. Everyone in her class had drawn names out of a box to exchange gifts at the end of the day. Iris drew the name of Bobbin Frye.

No one knew why he was named Bobbin. He was funny, had red hair, freckles and big teeth. Iris bought him a joke book. Mrs. Nilsen said, "We might as well give up on studying. Let's sing Carols and open our gifts." The gifts were under a small Christmas tree. The boys and girls would take home handmade ornaments and paper snowflakes they'd made.

When it was gift-opening time, Mrs. Nilsen passed around a tray of cookies. Iris reached for a wreath cookie and smelled it. "Oh, Mrs. Nilsen, you make the best molasses cookies! You are my favorite teacher."

Mrs. Nilsen beamed, "Iris, for that, you may pass out the presents."

Iris opened her gift. The card read, 'To Iris from Martin.' Martin sat in front of her. She poked him in the back. "How could you keep a secret so long?" There was an imitation pearl bracelet in the little box. "Martin," Iris said, poking him again, "This is beautiful. We were supposed to give silly gifts."

"My mother made me buy it," he admitted.

"I'll wear it for the pageant," said Iris.

The audience assembled. Iris' father pulled at the neck of his starched shirt. He stood and waved to Oscar and his father. Why had Oscar come to see a bunch of kids in bathrobes? Iris clutched her Bible as lights went out in the auditorium.

Iris thought when a lamb bleated and the audience laughed, was the best part of the play. The shepherds snickered. Her reading was last. She began, "And there were shepherds abiding in the fields, keeping watch over their flock by night."

The choir sang 'Away in the Manger.' Mary and Joseph took their places behind the manger. Two angels, Martha Rose, and a tiny girl from the first grade knelt on each side of the manger. As the curtains parted for a final scene, Iris noticed her little sister. Her halo was straight, arms crossed, as she smiled sweetly at the manger. Iris read, "But Mary kept all these things, and pondered them in her heart."

The choir walked down the aisles and sang, "Silent Night." Iris heard the audience join them. Then she was distracted by a movement. There was Martha Rose, waving wildly at the audience. The choir finished, 'Sleep in heavenly peace,' and the audience burst into laughter and applause.

As soon as the curtain closed, Miss Davis was on the spot. "Martha Rose, what were you thinking?"

"I love all the people," said Iris' little sister.

Her mother came back stage with a mad face. "Martha Rose," she began, but before she could continue, Miss Davis interrupted her. "Martha Rose 'loves all the people.' Isn't that what Christmas is about?"

Iris watched her mother struggle with her thoughts, until her mother said, "Martha Rose, I am so proud of you!" Martha Rose got hugs all evening.

Oscar came backstage. "Iris, turn around."

Iris did a pirouette.

"Gee!" Oscar wiped his forehead and repeated, "Gee!"

Then Iris' father was there hugging her. He picked up Martha Rose. She asked, "Daddy, was I good?"

"Monkey Doodle, you were perfect!"

Her mother mumbled, "That was one unorthodox angel."

This year Iris' family planned to go to Christmas Eve at Greenfield Lutheran church. On the morning of the twenty-fourth, Iris asked her mother, "Do you think we'll make it this year?"

Her mother said, "Yes, I do. I'm going to be careful and not slip on ice. No one has Scarlet Fever, no broken bones. After three years, we may make it to church on Christmas Eve!"

Iris dressed in front of the long mirror in her Mother's room She smoothed the red satin dress over her chest, and turned sideways to look again. Yes! Unmistakable signs of growth. Julie already wore a brassiere. Iris wondered if she'd ever develop.

She made a thick pony-tail of her hair and tied it with a white ribbon. Really, she was too old for pony tails. This dress deserved a special look. She pulled an end of the ribbon and her hair tumbled around her shoulders. She began to brush it. Her mother came into the room for her gloves. Iris said, "Mother, my hair!"

Her mother stood behind her. "I love your hair long. Leave it. Pull one side behind your ear."

Iris did. She looked in the mirror. "Oh, Mother!" Her hair was sleek against her head.

Her father called into the room, "If that doesn't take Oscar's breath away, he's hopeless!"

In church, Martha Rose whispered behind her hand to her big sister, "Oscar's looking at you."

The service passed in a beeswax-scented blur for Iris. Mrs. Nilsen had made the candles for the service. Iris thought she could do anything! Every heart in the little church seemed to beat together. The pastor's wife and a small girl sat behind them. Pastor Nilsen looked their way often. At the end of the service, Martha Rose was asleep. Her father picked her up in his arms. Iris thought, I wish someone could pick me up like that.

At the door Pastor Nilsen shook her father's hand and greeted her family. "Iris," he said, "you stood out like a flame! Merry Christmas to you all."

Earl Runs Like Fox and Oscar came up behind them. Oscar looked at her, closed his eyes, and took a deep breath. "Merry Christmas, Iris." He handed her a small box.

On the way home from church Iris asked her mother, "Who was the little girl with Mrs. Nilsen? Mrs. Nilsen was sniffling."

Her mother answered, "She's the Christmas miracle! Pastor Nilsen visits children's homes. He met Elsa a year ago. She's two. When she was ill, he prayed for her. She took his hand, and wouldn't let go. She was left at the home when she was a baby. She doesn't speak. Mrs. Nilsen went with him for his Thanksgiving visit. She didn't want to leave the little girl there. The adoption was final a week ago. They brought her home yesterday. Their life will never be the same. I hope Elsa can make friends. Being deaf is difficult at any age."

Iris said, "You mean, the Nilsens have a little girl, just like that?"

"Just like that," repeated her mother. "Much like your Uncle Luke and Anna."

Iris thought a while. "Who's going to teach tenth grade?"

Iris put the small box Oscar had given her in her coat pocket. When she got home, she took off her coat, and her father took it from her. I'll hang this up. I've got an armful of coats."

Iris was tucked in her bed, her light was out. She was warm, sleepy, and . . . remembered the box in her coat pocket! She thought about waiting until morning, then slipped out of bed, put her feet in her waiting slippers, and descended the stairs, creaking all the way.

Her father called out, "Who is making all that racket? People are trying to sleep here."

Iris heard her mother laugh. She opened the closet door, found her coat by feel, and searched first one, then the other pocket. Here it was. She took it and went back to her room. There was a green ribbon on the box, and she untied it. The box was small, about the size for a bracelet. Inside was cotton. Iris removed it, and there sat a rock. Not any rock, a smooth lake rock. At the bottom of the box was a note in Oscar's handwriting. My mother found this rock when she was a young girl. If you look closely, it is in the shape of a heart, sort of. She kept it in the window by the sink where she could see it every day and remember the lake. I want to take you there. We will return the rock together. Your Friend, Oscar.

Iris held the rock in her palm. It fit her hand perfectly. She put the rock under her pillow.

Chapter Five

JANUARY

Iris dawdled over her oatmeal. One elbow was on the table, her hand supporting her chin. "Oh, Mother, January is long and dull. Even Muffin and Biscuit are bored." Both cats slept in the kitchen rocker.

Her mother smiled at her. "That's because Christmas is so much fun. January is calm. I could never keep December's pace!"

"Calm isn't the word. Dull, dull, dull, is. Nothing happens in January except snow."

"I wish I'd hear from Annie Carlson. I wonder how Christmas was for them. I hope she's glad life is calmer."

"Mother, you do remember it took us years to feel at home. You could call her. They have their first telephone."

"Iris, I want her to feel settled, and write or call first. I don't want to intrude."

"I think about them a lot," said Iris.

"I do, too," said her mother.

"Mother, suppose she's waiting for you to call her! This is ridiculous. Here you are, missing your friend, you are a grown up waiting for the other to call."

Iris heard her brother from his room calling, "I, I, I!"

That was his word for Iris. Martha Rose was "Muf," Merry was "Whee," he called his father, "Da" and his mother, "Mum-mum."

Iris said, "I'll change Ben, and bring him down if you call Mrs. Carlson."

When Iris came downstairs with Ben dressed and happy her mother stood by the phone. "Did you call her," she asked.

"I did. I felt like I was talking to a stranger. What a short conversation! Something's not right." She took off her apron and sat in a kitchen chair.

Ben pointed at the door, "Go! Go!"

Iris got his snowsuit ready. "O.K. we'll go!"

"Go! Go!" Ben said with a grin.

Cookie sat by the door and thumped her tail. She was ready to play.

Iris set off for the first day of school of the new year with a heavy heart. No one knew who their teacher would be. If Miss Davis knew, she wasn't telling. Neither was Mrs. Nilsen. Julie and Iris planned to meet at the school door and walk to class together.

Julie bounded up the steps. Iris said, "What took you so long?"

"Have you seen our new teacher," asked Julie, breathless.

"No. Miss Davis went in our room a few minutes ago. She's still there."

Julie stopped in her tracks, "Oh, no! You don't think she's our new teacher, do you?"

Iris groaned. "I never thought of that." Her shoulders sagged.

The two girls walked into their room. Most of the class was there. Miss Davis stood by Mrs. Nilsen's old desk chatting about Christmas. The bell rang, and the students took their seats. Miss Davis spoke to the class, "Good morning, boys and girls!"

The class responded, "Good morning, Miss Davis."

There was a gleam in the principal's eyes.

"You know the good news about Mrs. Nilsen. Elsa is one lucky little girl. I know you agree with me."

The class beamed a smile for her.

She continued, "I think you'll believe a genie has transformed your classroom when you meet your new teacher. I must say, I never thought I'd hire this young man.

He was a student here. Class, please great your," she

cleared her throat, "teacher, Mr. Luke Andersen!" Miss Davis stood aside and Uncle Luke jumped out of the coat closet.

Iris gasped, "Uncle Luke!"

He looked her way and said, "Professor Andersen, if you please." He looked at the classroom. "The rest of the class may call me Uncle Luke!"

Miss Davis looked uneasy. "Luke Andersen, I can still keep you after school, you know."

The class laughed, and Luke and Miss Davis shook hands. He said, "This is a dream come true!"

Iris thought, it certainly is!

Miss Davis was right. The classroom was transformed in a hurry. The students moved their desks. Uncle Luke unscrewed the bolts from the floor and they turned their desks to face the windows. Two boys carried in a tall book case and placed it where the map of Minnesota used to hang. Several students carried in boxes of books and pads of unlined paper. Iris and Julie moved the teacher's desk to the back of the room and shoved it against the wall. Uncle Luke brought a stool to the front of the room and sat on it. Everybody took a seat. He sat and stared at them. Then he said, "Let's go to lunch. I'm hungry."

After lunch he asked the class to dress warmly and they would play follow the leader. Iris and her class followed him down the steps into the crunchy frozen snow. Iris and Julie hurried to keep up with his long-legged stride. Julie asked, "Uncle Luke, where are we going?"

"I don't know! I wanted to see how it would feel to get up and walk out of school."

The class followed him to the edge of town. He stood and looked at them, his gloved hands on his hips. "Tomorrow we begin an alphabet lunch."

Bobbin spoke up, "What's that?"

"An alphabet lunch. Everybody has to bring something to eat that starts with an "A" tomorrow, "B" on Tuesday, "C" on Wednesday, and so on."

Julie asked, "Did you make that up?"

"I did!" he said proudly. "Let's go back to school. There is only one way to walk, and that is v-e-r-y slowly."

Bobbin asked, "Won't we be late?"

"For what," asked Uncle Luke.

Bobbin's face turned red. "Miss Davis won't like this."

Uncle Luke walked over to Bobbin, leaned down, and looked in his face. "Bobbin, I wasn't making fun of you. I've never taught ninth grade. I won't go about this job like Mrs. Nilsen did. I do have a reason in this little escape though, and I will tell you about it when we get back to our room. Okay?"

Bobbin nodded, "Okay."

Uncle Luke instructed his class, "Keep your eyes open, your ears keen, and don't say a word until we are together in our classroom again."

The class watched as he began to shamble along the road. He stopped and looked into snow filled fields. So did they. He stopped and looked at clouds. So did they.

Iris wondered what her class looked like to neighbors who might see them. Julie walked next to Uncle Luke. She walked in a perfectly straight line. All of a sudden she did a little dance and threw her arms in the air. Uncle Luke saw her and imitated her gesture. Soon the whole class was dancing down the center of the street behind their new teacher.

An hour later they dragged into their classroom. Their faces glowed from the cold air. Uncle Luke handed Bobbin a stack of papers and had him put one on each desk. Iris looked at her paper. At the top of the page in her Uncle's handwriting were these words, The Netherlands. Vincent Van Gogh.

He explained, "Each of you has a country and the name of a person from that country on their desk. For two weeks we'll come to our desks after lunch and work on our projects. We'll go to the library in Rochester in a week and spend the whole day. At the end of the two weeks we will share what we learned."

Julie raised and hand. "Do you want us to write a paper?

How many pages?"

"If you choose to write a paper, fine. If you want to draw a map, or a picture, wonderful. Some of you have the name of an author. You might want to read a poem to the class, or a play. If you have an artist's name, you could show us a picture, or paint one like theirs. Later we can talk about ideas. I want you to be a part of this experiment."

Iris spoke up, "We've never had an assignment like this."

"Good," smiled Uncle Luke.

Iris saw her mother in the yard taking sheets frozen hard off the line. She ran to her. "Mother! I can't believe you would keep such a secret from me."

Her mother grinned. "It wasn't easy. Your Uncle Luke was so excited he could hardly stand to come to the house. He said he was afraid he'd blurt it out, or you'd know."

"You should have seen him. He jumped out of the coat closet!"

Her mother burst into laughter. "I hope you learn something this year!"

Iris responded, "We will. We will. We do Arithmetic and Grammar in the morning, then after lunch we have projects. We're going to the library in Rochester next week! Can you believe it?" Iris did a full circle twirl in the icy yard.

"Any you thought January would be dull!"

"It won't be. Tomorrow everything in my lunch has to start with "A." Apple and, oh, something. Then on Wednesday, "B", bacon sandwich and brownies. How's that?" Iris's imagination was in full swing. 'C', what could she bring that started with a 'C'? Chocolate!

The new book shelf in Iris' classroom was full geography books, poetry, biographies, plays and picture books of artist's work. Iris began to read about Vincent Van Gogh. She poured over copies of his paintings in Uncle's books and at the library in Rochester. She told her mother, "I can't decide if I like the paintings or not, but I can't stop looking at them. When I'm not looking at the book, I see them in my mind."

Julie was studying England, and the works of William Shakespeare. She amazed Iris with her ability to memorize poetry and lines from plays. Julie told Uncle Luke that she would present part of A Midsummer Night's Dream that you shall never forget. She had a new way of tilting her chin up and looking down her nose. Iris thought it was classy. Her best friend was an actress. On the way home from school one day, Julie turned to face North and said, "Blow, blow, thou winter wind, Thou are not so unkind as man's ingratitude; Thy tooth is not so keen, because thou are not seen, Although thy breath be rude. . . That's Shakespeare! Isn't it grand!"

Julie was developing an English accent.

When Iris read about Vincent Van Gogh, and his tempermental personality, she thought of Gunther Carlson. When she discovered that Van Gogh had been in a mental institution, cut off his ear, and committed suicide, she became uneasy. She kept her fear to herself. She did continue to question her mother about the Carlsons.

A dark evening in late January, her father answered the telephone. As he talked the family grew quiet, even Ben. Into the black receiver he said, "Calm down. Take a deep breath. Talk to me, Annie."

Iris' mother jumped up and ran to her husband's side. He put his hand over the telephone and said, "Gunther's gone. Annie's hysterical."

Her mother took the phone. "Annie! Oh, Annie! Listen to me. This is Laura Ellen. I'm coming to St. Sebastian tonight. Yes. I'm leaving as soon as I get a few things ready. I knew something was wrong when I called and you wouldn't talk to me. I can't wait to see you. Hold on tight. I'm on my way." She hung up the telephone and looked at her family. "You can get along without me. Annie is desperate."

Iris asked, “How long has he been gone?”

Her father answered, “Two days.”

Iris was distressed. “Mother, we have to find him,” she cried. Her mind raced as she thought of Vincent Van Gogh checking himself into a mental institution. How could Mr. Carlson leave his family? Vincent didn’t have a family, only a brother.

Merry began to weep. “It’s so cold!” she cried. “What will he do if he’s outside?”

She pulled herself into her mother’s lap. “Do you think he has a blanket? Do you think he took his easel and paints? Where would he hide?”

Martha Rose turned to her father, “I let him wear my hat. He laughed when he put it on. Why would he go away?”

Iris’s father hugged the child, “Oh, honey, no one knows but Mr. Carlson.”

Chapter Six

FEBRUARY

Gunther Carlson did not return. Iris and her mother agonized over his whereabouts. Uncle Luke wanted to look for him, but kept his responsibility of teaching ninth grade. Iris included Mr. Carlson in her prayers at night. She earnestly prayed he was warm and would come back to his family and paint again. She had nightmares that he lay shivering in the dark.

One evening her mother announced that since Mr. Carlson was not teaching at the college, the family had to move out of faculty housing. She said, “Annie feels helpless. She doesn’t have enough money to rent a place. Since Gunther has been working, she hasn’t done any sewing. She wants to return to Harmony with her children. They liked it here.”

Merry spoke up, “Someone else is living over the hardware store. They can’t go back.”

Iris thought a while. “When Vincent Van Gogh died, his family had to sell his paintings to settle his debts. Could Mrs. Carlson sell some paintings?”

Her mother looked shocked, “Annie would never sell them! They’re family pictures.”

Her husband patted her shoulder. “You are passionate about those paintings, aren’t you? Annie may not have any other choice. It will be a sad day, that’s for sure.”

Iris asked, “What about the paintings her friends have stored in Norway?”

Her mother and father exchanged glances.

Her mother said, “Let’s get Annie and her children back to Harmony, then we’ll make decisions together.”

When Iris returned home from school Monday, a black car was parked at the back of the farmhouse. She had to see who it was first, then she'd spend some time with Joshua and War Bonnet in the barn. She'd brush them good.

Father Leo from the Catholic Church sat at the kitchen table with her mother and father. He wore a black suit and black shirt with a round white collar around his neck. It looked uncomfortable! Her mother looked up as she came in. She had a smile on her face.

"Father Leo's found a place for Annie and the children," she said. "They're returning Saturday!"

Iris asked, "Where?"

The priest answered, "There's an abandoned farm house two miles out of town. Members of the church don't want to sell it, but they'll rent it for a small amount. It's ideal for the Carlsons. The congregation has paid the first two months' rent. It needs some fixing up," he added with a grimace.

Her mother was excited. She held up a key. "Father Leo gave me the key. We can sweep and dust and get some food in before Saturday. The woman's circle at our church is going to meet there in two days."

Father Leo said, "When the women from our church and your church get finished, Annie Carlson won't have to cook or clean for a month. We remember her generous spirit." He turned to Iris' father and shook his hand. "I'm grateful you called. Here we are, Lutherans and Catholics working together." His eyes crinkled with a grin.

Iris knew that Annie Carlson, who'd grown up in Wisconsin in a Lutheran family, had met Gunther in France. He was a Catholic, and Annie joined the church so they could be married there. Now the Carlson family attended the Catholic church. Father Leo said the boys were the best acolytes he'd ever known.

The next day Iris' mother, the three Andersen girls, and Julie and her mother met at the Carlson's future home. The trunks of both cars were full of brooms, mops, floor wax, and ammonia for window washing. Laughing Sky had taken Ben to play with Anna at their cabin.

As her mother drove the rutted road to the farmhouse, Iris's heart sank. She leaned over the front seat and sighed. "Father Leo did say 'abandoned'."

The house was unpainted; boards weathered gray. The porch sagged and there were no steps. Her mother unlocked the front door and remarked, "This is a handsome door. It needs paint, but look at it!"

The panels were carved with spirals. Iris said, "Mrs. Carlson will probably paint it yellow!"

They entered the house. The living room was desolate. Tall dirty widows looked out onto snowy fields. The ceilings were high. It was freezing. There were cobwebs in every corner. Out of one window Iris saw an old barn and a shed that leaned towards it. There was a wood cooking stove in the kitchen. Next to the kitchen was a huge room. Wallpaper hung in gaping tongues from the plastered walls. Her mother said, "I declare!" It was all she needed to say.

Merry called from upstairs, "Come up here!"

They trooped up a steep set of stairs. There were three bedrooms. The largest room had a fireplace on one wall. Her mother walked about upstairs, then downstairs, and called up, "There's no bathroom or furnace!"

Mrs. Gonner said, "If we're going to work here, we need some heat. There'll be a wood pile out back. Come on, girls."

Julie began to quote, "When icicles hang by the wall, and Dick the shepherd blows his nail, and Tom bears logs into the hall, and milk comes frozen home in pail, when blood is nipped and ways be foul, the nightly sings the staring owl, To-who, To-whit, To-who, a merry note, while greasy Joan doth keel the pot!"

Mrs. Gonner gave a great hoot of laughter, "My daughter, the Shakespeare lover! God bless your Uncle Luke."

The girls pushed snow off the wood pile and began to carry

logs and small limbs to the kitchen stove. Julie placed twigs and bits of wood chips on the bottom of the kitchen stove. Iris' mother found dry wood stacked in the barn and when she added it to the bits and pieces, the fire roared to life. She suggested, "Let's close doors so the kitchen stays warm and we can work here."

Iris asked, "Mother, may Julie and I pull the wallpaper off the wall in the downstairs bedroom? It looks so awful."

"Yes, you can do whatever you want. Every room needs work. We'll have to work fast. Take these rags and wipe the window sills to get the worst of the dust off them, then we can wash the inside of the windows when we melt some snow."

Merry said, "We can add the wallpaper to the fire!"

"That's a pretty good idea," admitted Iris.

"Where's Martha Rose," her mother asked.

"Probably getting in trouble," said Merry.

Iris opened the kitchen door. Tracks made by small boots led to the barn. "I'll get her," she said. She followed the footprints to the barn. Up close the structure looked more sturdy than it did from a distance. She called, "Martha Rose, come inside and get warm!"

"Iris, look what I found."

Martha Rose was in one of the horse stalls. She leaned out and waved to her sister. "Come see."

Iris followed her sister's voice. Martha Rose stood in front of a large round mirror covered in cobwebs. She wondered aloud, "Who would put a mirror in a horse stall?"

Iris tried to pick up the mirror. "Uff-da," she said. Martha Rose took one side of the mirror. They trudged through the snow with it.

When their mother opened the door for them she blinked at the sight. "We'll clean that. I know where it belongs." There was a light circle over the fireplace in the living room just the size of the mirror. The nail was still there.

Martha Rose hollered, "I found it; I get to clean it!"

Her mother said, "What a treasure. Let's take it into the

kitchen where we'll be warm. You can clean it there. We'll hang it before we leave today."

"There's other things, a rolled up rug and two black chairs," said Martha Rose.

Together Iris and Julie said, "Let's go," and ran out the kitchen door. They returned carrying a rug between them like a long pole.

Julie's mother said, "I'll sweep the living room floor then mop it. We'll lay the rug after we hang the mirror. It seems like this room is getting a workout instead of the warm kitchen. Tomorrow we put a fire in here also." She had a large soapy rag. She rubbed the top of the mantle piece, and the wood turned from dirty gray to white. "It looks like home already," said Merry.

The rug was muted red with a dark blue pattern. Iris' mother stood with her hands on her hips. "Lord love us, we have an oriental rug in Harmony, Minnesota!"

Mrs. Gonner announced, "Time for a break!"

Martha Rose and Merry carried the two black chairs inside and put them in front of the kitchen's wood stove. Iris and Julie's mother sank into them. Iris poured milk for everyone, and passed around a sack of almond cookies. They would have to take the glasses home to wash them. The pump in the kitchen sink didn't work. Mrs. Gonner cleaned the counter, pie safe, and floor.

Iris' mother said, "I'll get Horace to work on this pump. It probably needs to be primed. Annie must have running water when she gets here."

Martha Rose said, "I like this house." She said 'like' real loud.

"I do too," agreed her mother. "We have one more hour of light. Iris, why don't you and Julie start on the wallpaper in the bedroom. We can open the door between it and the kitchen and let in some warmth in there. The kitchen is cozy, don't you think?"

"It feels good in here," said Mrs. Gonner. "Girls, you're off to pull paper."

Iris and Julie had an easy time. The pale strips came away and lay in curls on the floor. Iris said, "This is fun! I can hardly wait for the Carlsons to come. Annie will have one room green, one blue, one yellow before you know it!"

"And one red," added Julie.

Iris' nightmares about Gunther Carlson continued. The dream repeated itself. The next Tuesday at school, Uncle Luke talked about the history of Harmony. He told how the Ojibway Indians used the nearby limestone caves for rituals, and Iris's nightmare popped into her head. Terrified, she jumped up and ran from the room.

Her uncle found her cringing at the school's front door, gazing out of the frosted window onto the barren school yard.

"Iris, are you all right?"

"She wrapped her arms around herself and chewed her lower lip. "My nightmare came back right there in class when you talked about the caves." Her wavery voice surprised her.

Her Uncle Luke led her by the elbow to sit next to him on Miss Davis's bench. "Iris, tell me what's going on."

She took a deep breath. "I've been dreaming about Mr. Carlson since he left. He's in the dark, he's cold, and he shivers. It doesn't sound like much, but it scares me. Today when you mentioned caves, I got scared of them. You know I've been afraid of them since Daddy fell, and the bats came flying at us, . . ." She shivered and her Uncle put his arm around her.

"Have you told your mother," he asked.

"I haven't told anyone. We're worried about Annie and all those children. Father Leo found a house, and we've started cleaning it, you know all that, but what about Mr. Carlson? Who's looking for him? Do you think he'll come back?"

Her uncle sighed and rubbed the knees of his dark trousers, "Iris, I have a feeling he will. We can't hurry him. The best thing we can do is help his family. I know the Lutherans and Catholics are praying for the same thing, and that's a miracle in itself."

Iris asked, "Do you know why he would leave the college?"

"It was probably too many changes too fast; too much responsibility. Gunther's an artist. He needs to paint," said her uncle.

"Do you think he'll try to kill himself like Vincent Van Gogh," asked Iris.

Her Uncle pulled her close. "You've thought of everything, haven't you? When a person is sad and confused, they do scary things. Let's hope Gunther can pull himself up and return to his family and Harmony." He hugged her quickly. "Let's go back before Bobbin Frye takes my job. I left him in charge."

The day the Carlsons returned to Harmony was a bright cold one. Iris, her mother, and sisters, Oscar, Julie, and her mother were at the new Carlson house. They had a fire going in each fireplace, and the kitchen cookstove. Mr. Crocker came to the door and asked for help carrying in a few things. Iris, Oscar, and Julie went out with him. Mr. Crocker laughed when he saw Iris' face. There were three cans of paint in the trunk of his car, yellow, blue, and red. Iris said, "You thought of everything!"

Oscar carried in a large porcelain chamber pot. "Really, Mr. Crocker, you did think of everything!" he said.

When her mother opened the door and saw Oscar and his burden, she also laughed. "You are a brilliant and practical man, Mr. Crocker!"

Julie held up a basket. "Look, nails and wire to hang pictures! Just what Mrs. Carlson will need."

Laura Ellen said, "Oh, I hope Annie will get to save a few of Gunther's paintings."

"What are you talking about," asked Mr. Crocker in surprise.

Iris' mother explained, "Annie has decided to sell some of Gunther's paintings. There are a large number of watercolors and oils on their way from Europe. The sale will be at the Catholic church in two weeks. Annie advertised in the St. Paul paper, and Horace took out an ad in the New York Times! If the pictures from France don't arrive in time, Annie will sell family pictures. I know she's holding her breath."

The Lutheran and Catholic women's guilds had been there the day before putting final touches in the rooms. The kitchen windows were framed with white curtains held back with yellow ribbon. The two black chairs Martha Rose found were in the kitchen. Annie's chairs and table would arrive today.

"Look at this," said Julie. She opened the pantry door.

Oscar and Iris joined her in the crowded space. There were jars of tomatoes, bread and butter pickles, green beans, limas, sauerkraut, grape jelly and rhubarb sauce. A crate held potatoes and onions. Julie touched a jar of plum jam. "This will make Annie sad."

"Sad?" questioned Oscar.

"Yes. She'll feel like she can't pay everyone back. I almost wish we hadn't made it so nice," she finished.

Iris said, "People like her. They can't do enough for her."

"I hear trucks," said Oscar. "Time to unload."

Iris' mother stood on the porch. Annie Carlson jumped out of Earl's truck and ran to her friend's open arms. Iris could hear Annie's sobs before her mother led her into the house. Iris's mother was patting Annie's hair saying, "There, there, hush now, hush."

Mr. Crocker stood in the doorway turning his hat in his hands.

Oscar opened the door to the Andersen's car, and Lily hopped out. "We're home!" she announced in a loud voice.

Yes. They were.

Chapter Seven

MARCH

Iris and Julie sat on the top slat of Joshua's stall. On the floor, Oscar held a blocky hoof between his knees, cleaning it with a curved blade.

While Oscar worked, the girls talked about school. Julie said, "Lars is thin and pale. He doesn't look at anyone."

"He didn't look at anyone before, except when he drew them," added Iris. Then she asked her favorite question, "If you were Gunther Carlson, where would you be?"

Julie heaved an exasperated sigh, "Oh, Iris! You are not going to find Gunther Carlson. If he's smart, he went somewhere warm, Florida, maybe."

Oscar looked up from the horse's hoof. "I don't think so," he said quietly.

Iris jumped down into the stall. "Oscar, what do you know?"

Oscar straightened up. "You leap to conclusions. I don't know anything. I have a feeling," he said.

Iris looked him in the eye.

A car crunched down the frozen drive and Julie hopped from her perch. She pulled her scarf close. "That's Daddy. He always comes early. See you tomorrow, Iris. So long, Oscar!"

Oscar called after Julie, "Your father comes early because he misses you."

Julie hollered from the door, "I know!"

Iris shivered as a cold wind blew into the barn. "Why is it getting cold again? Spring begins in March at home, wherever that is." She watched Oscar pick up another hoof. "Oscar, why did you say you have a feeling about Mr. Carlson? Why would you say that if it didn't mean anything?"

Oscar shrugged his shoulders and stood. "It's a hunch." He looked at Iris. "A lantern and horse blanket are missing from our barn."

"Is that it," asked Iris.

"There were footprints around the barn and up to our porch, but they stopped at the back steps."

Iris's eyes widened. "Did you follow the footprints?"

"I might know where they go," answered Oscar.

Iris grabbed his arm. "If you know, we have to go! We need to bring Gunther back. He went to the caves, didn't he? I dream of him shivering in the dark."

"We shouldn't interfere with Mr. Carlson. I don't know he's there. He needs to decide to come back on his own. I remember you said you'd never go back to the caves after your father's accident."

"I'd go for Gunther Carlson," said Iris. "Tomorrow you and I will go. I'll take a loaf of bread, cheese and blankets. Don't tell anyone."

Oscar said, "It's too cold. The snow is deep."

"I'll wear the snow shoes we found in the tractor shed," said Iris.

"All right, if you insist. I'll come after school. What are you going to tell your mother?"

"I'll say you're teaching me to use snowshoes. That's the truth anyway."

"Or part of it," said Oscar.

"Tomorrow we'll do it. Shake."

Oscar took her hand. "We'll do it together." He gave her hand one hard shake and continued to hold it.

Oscar knocked on Iris' kitchen door at three the next afternoon. Her mother stood at the ironing board watching her daughter wrap a scarf around her neck. "There, Mother," said Iris. Only her eyes showed and they glinted fiercely.

Her mother laughed, "I can't be angry when you look at me

like that." She hugged Iris. "You feel like a dumpling." She turned to Oscar, "I know you two are up to something. Promise me you won't let my oldest do anything dangerous."

"Promise," said Oscar.

"Promise," said Iris in a muffled voice. "Mother, how many hours do you spend doing that?" She pointed to the ironing board and pile of shirts and blouses her mother dampened and folded until they looked like loaves of bread.

"I'm going to teach you this spring," her mother remarked.

Oscar knelt on the porch and tied rawhide straps around Iris' boots. She took a few waddling steps in the snow shoes and whispered, "I have a sack of food and a quilt behind the barn. What's in your pack?"

Oscar shifted the weight of a canvas pack on his back. He grinned, "Stuff. Let's go."

The walk to the river was strenuous in snowshoes. Iris remember how easy the trek had been two years ago. At least the sun was shining today. The thermometer on the barn read twenty-seven degrees above zero. Maybe spring was on the way. She never imagined that twenty-seven would feel good. She began to puff and blow. Oscar turned around. She waved to him. "Keep on going. I'm fine!"

Oscar pointed, "We're near the river."

Iris looked at the white scene. A row of trees marked the river's edge. Ahead and to the right was the snowy incline to the caves. Her heart began to thud and she knew it wasn't from exertion. She felt a tingle of fear. "Oscar!" She could hear a raspy sound in her voice. "Oscar!"

Her turned and smiled. "You look like you saw a grizzly."

Iris leaned on her friend and took a deep breath. "I, I, can't," she cried.

Oscar leaned into her. "You don't have to. Come stand inside the cave where you'll be in the sunlight. I'll go in. How about that?" He put one arm around her and pulled her to him in a quick hug.

Her smile was weak.

"Don't give me that silly look. We don't have a lot of time. Stand inside out of the wind, all right?"

Iris nodded her head and followed Oscar into the mouth of the cave. Snow had blown around the entrance. The two friends climbed a small mound of ice and ducked their heads to enter the cave. Oscar lit his lantern and continued into the cave. Iris called, "Hurry," as he rounded a bend and was out of sight.

She listened to his footsteps recede and squatted down to rest, keeping her eyes on the cave's bright entrance. A rock fell nearby and she shot to her feet, trembling. There were no foot prints or signs that Gunther Carlson used the cave as a hiding place. Iris sighed in disappointment. Footsteps alerted her to Oscar's return. "Oscar? Oscar?"

His familiar voice replied, "Coming," and her heart calmed it's anxious pace.

As soon as Oscar appeared around the bend Iris began, "Oh, I'm so glad to see you! A rock fell and I almost . . ."

"He's here," said Oscar.

Iris grabbed the bag of food she'd brought. "Did you talk to him? How did he get in if there're no footprints?"

"Will you give me a chance?"

"Sorry."

"He's here. His lantern is warm. It's from our barn. He obviously heard us and blew it out. Our horse blanket is here, too."

"Did you tell him who we are?" asked Iris.

"I did. I called and called. I said that we'd leave food. I told him we wouldn't tell anyone else where he is."

"Is that all?"

"What else is there?"

Iris took his flashlight, "Oscar, you left out everything!" She began to walk into the cave.

"Iris, what are you doing?"

Iris continued to walk. Just around the bend she stopped and put her sack on the ground. She began to talk. "Mr.

Carlson? This is Iris, your friend. Annie, Lily and the boys moved back to Harmony. Except for missing you, they're fine." She waited. Silence was full of the sound of her breathing and the distant trickle of water.

Oscar took her arm, "Come on, Iris."

She continued, "This Saturday Annie is going to sell paintings at the Catholic church at noon. Harmony is not the same without you." She turned to Oscar. "Do you think he's all right? Could he understand me?"

He took her gloved hand. "We have to go. Mr. Carlson will make up his mind. You Uncle Luke is right. Gunther Carlson will come back when he's ready."

On Saturday Iris' family drove into town. There was not a parking space on Main Street, or the side streets near St. Gabriel's. Her father let out a grunt, "Would you look at this!"

He found a space two blocks away. As they walked to the church, Merry read license plates. "Look, New York, Iowa, Michigan. Daddy, I don't know how these people even found Harmony!"

"I don't either," quipped her mother.

Her father answered, "Let's hope they brought money."

When they entered the fellowship hall, Iris looked for Oscar. He and his father stood in front of a spring painting of wheat field outside of town. Iris walked up to Oscar and tapped him on the shoulder. The two of them stood in front of the painting. There was a 'Sold' sign on it. Lars saw Oscar and Iris and headed towards them. "Come," he said. He led them to the opposite side of the room. There was Mr. Crocker's autumn wheat field painting with a 'Sold' sign attached. Next to the bright painting was a small gilt-framed oil of a lake surrounded by snow covered mountains. "Norway," Lars said. "Sold," he added.

Iris said, "Lars, this is wonderful." She grabbed his hand and began to shake it.

"So far, no one will buy the family collection. Two days

ago paintings arrived from Norway and France. All sold! There's a collector from New York. Mother's tired and ready to go home, but people want to stand and look."

Iris had never hear Lars say so many words at once.

Oscar said wistfully, "Mr. Crocker's wheat field was my favorite. I'll miss it. Maybe your father will paint another one." Oscar stopped talking and stood stone still.

Iris and Lars followed his stare.

The crowd parted to allow a tall white-haired gentleman to enter the room. Gunther Carlson took off his floppy hat and held it over his heart. "Ja. I come home," he said. "Home." He bent his head.

In a moment of stillness Father Leo said a quiet, "Thanks be to God."

Gunther was swallowed up by his children who grabbed his arms and hugged whatever part they could find of their father. Mrs. Carlson came forward in the chaos and put her arm through her husband's arm. The crowd grew quiet. She looked up at the artist and said, "We start again." She repeated, "Start again."

Gunther and his family moved towards the door. The crowd parted respectfully. Annie Carlson turned at the doorway. Her eyes were bright, and her smile trembled. Her voice, though, was strong and clear. "We will receive guests after seven this evening in our new home." Iris' father hurried to drive them to their farmhouse.

After their dinner, the Andersens drove to the Carlson's gray house. Luke's car was there, and Iris spotted Mr. Crocker's pickup truck. She hoped tourists wouldn't barge in. As soon as her family got out of the car, Earl and Oscar drove up. The two families stepped onto the porch together. The steps were new. Iris smiled at the yellow- green door. It opened and Gunther Carlson waved them inside.

The big front room was transformed. The furniture was gone, rug, too. Candles reflected in the windows. An easel stood in one corner of the room. A smaller one held a charcoal sketch. She crossed the room to get a better look.

Gunther Carlson waved his arms around the room. "My studio. *Velkhommen*!"

Annie stood next to him. "This room gets wonderful light. I knew Gunther would love it. The day we moved in I cleared it of furniture and curtains and set up his easels. Gunther has a place to work!"

Iris' mother moved forward with Benjamin in her arms. The baby saw his friend and cooed. Gunther's face brightened and he answered Ben with, "Ahh, ahh," and took the child in his arms. Ben pulled his beard and laughed out loud.

Uncle Luke spoke from the kitchen doorway. "We have coffee and warm gingerbread. Help yourself."

The neighbors moved into the warm kitchen. Iris, Oscar, and Lars stayed in the studio. "This is yours, isn't it, Lars," she asked. The sketch was a bare tree with branches that stretched to the sky, and roots that reached to the ground.

Oscar said, "It looks like a mirror."

Lars said, "It is a mirror. You have good eyes, Oscar. My father and I work together. First time," he added. "Now, cake!"

When the three of them entered the kitchen, Gunther Carlson came straight to them. "Hear me!" he said. Conversation stopped. The artist stood in silence before the crowd. His eyes searched for and found his wife. She moved across the kitchen and put her hand on his arm. Gunther cleared his throat. "I come back." He put one hand on Iris' shoulder, and one on Oscar's. He embraced them both. "I thank you."

Iris saw her mother and father exchange glances. Well, Iris would tell them about her return trip to the cave . . . one day.

Chapter Eight

APRIL

Lars came to the Andersen farm on a regular basis. When Iris saw his red bicycle near the barn, she knew he was sketching Joshua and War Bonnet. He'd done several sketches of Snowball who had grown from lamb to sheep in a hurry. Merry had the pictures of Snowball in her room. She spent almost as much time sketching as Lars did. Her sketches of Snowball showed the bulky sheep with a grin. Do sheep grin? Merry's did. Lars spent hours sketching chickens. There was one of Cheeky Chick glaring at him from her nest. Right now, he was fascinated with Joshua. Lars had pages of the horse's eyes, flanks, head, chest. One day she asked, "What's special about an old horse?"

Lars didn't look up from his work. "Joshua has nobility."

There was a stack of sketches sitting on a hay bale. "What are you going to do with those," she asked.

"I'm practicing to enter a competition. I'm going to send a charcoal sketch of Joshua." He looked up at Iris. "If I win, I'll study art for a year in France. A lot of artists will enter, though."

"None of them work as hard as you do," Iris said. "I'm going to help you win."

Lars raised his head, "You?"

Iris was on her way to the house. She returned with a tall reading lamp which she plugged into the only electrical socket in the barn. "Thanks," said Lars.

Iris left. She returned with a glass of milk and a handful of cookies. "What else do you need," she asked.

Lars laughed at his friend. "If I don't win, you'll feel as bad as I do. I tell you what. I'll let you decided which sketch to send."

"You will? Honest?"

"You have my word," promised Lars.

Iris sat at the kitchen table with her mother and Lars. She looked from one sketch to another. She pointed. "This one. This is the way Joshua looks at me when I come home from school. It's like he's asking, 'What took you so long? I've been waiting all day!" She spoke with a deep rumbling voice.

"That's the one, then," declared Lars. He gathered his sketches in his canvas case. "Will you still come and draw," asked Iris' mother.

"I'll be back. I want to draw our farmhouse before mother fixes the rest of the porch. When it's perfect, there'll be no reason to draw it."

Iris asked, "Why do you do black and white sketches? Why don't you paint?"

Lars thought a moment. "Color isn't everything to me like it is for my father. Shapes are. Lines are. Positive and negative space is. Look, it's going to rain. I'd better ride home. Thanks for the cookies, the lamp, and Joshua. I think he knew I was sketching him. He would sigh, then not move a muscle. He's the best model I ever had."

Iris' mother said, "Lars, I hate to disappoint you, but that's the way he is. He moves about every half hour. Our Joshua is an elderly gentleman and getting lazier every day."

That evening Iris bent over her Arithmetic homework. Her books were spread on the kitchen table. She heard thunder and saw flashes from lightning as she studied. Merry sat across from her spelling words out loud. "C-A-L-E-N-D-, Iris is it AR or ER," she asked. She looked at her book, "Oh, it's A-R!" she shouted.

Iris gave her an exasperated look. "I'm trying to think. Let mother call your words."

"Iris, you're the best speller I know," said Merry.

Martha Rose came in the room with Cookie close behind her. She pulled up a chair. "Hi, Iris."

Iris said, "At this rate I'll never get my homework done. I'm going to the barn. Joshua and War Bonnet can't talk." She gathered her books and called into the living room. "Mother, I'm going to study in the barn. Call out Merry's words. I'm busy."

Iris ran from the house to the barn, pulled open the heavy door, and hurried inside. She shook rain from her hair and flicked on the light in the barn. She looked towards Joshua's stall, but there was no sign of him. She walked over to the door of his stall and saw him on his side in the hay. "Joshua," she called. The horse lifted his head. "Are you all right?"

She opened the door and went in. "You must be tired after all that posing." She stroked the horse's neck. "I've got to finish my homework." She sat on a bale of hay outside his stall and finished her work. "I wish you could learn my times tables for me," she said. "I'll get daddy to look in on you before he goes to bed. Sweet dreams." She closed his gate, turned off the weak light, and ran through the rain to the house.

Her father was telling Martha Rose her bedtime story, so Iris told her mother, "Joshua was on his side in the hay. Is he all right?"

"He's old and tired. He's fine. I'm sure of it."

"Would you ask daddy to look at him before he goes to bed; make sure he's all right?" Iris insisted

"I will, Iris, but he's being lazy," said her mother.

The next morning Iris' father hurried the girls into the car. Rain came down in buckets. He promised to drive them to the bus stop and wait with them until it arrived. Iris asked, "Daddy, did you look at Joshua last night?"

"I did. If every farmer worried when a horse laid down, Dr. Beard would be a millionaire. I'll keep an eye on Joshua. He was standing up waiting for his breakfast this morning."

"Did he eat," asked Iris.

"I did not stay to watch," her father replied.

Martha Rose shouted, "Here's the bus!"

Iris gave her father one last pleading look. "Daddy, please, please check on Joshua while I'm at school."

Her father stroked her hair, "I promise."

At the end of the day Iris ran home from the bus stop. Rain poured off her head and down her neck, but she didn't care. She stopped the minute she saw both doors to the barn open and the veterinarian's car parked outside.

Her father and the doctor stood at Joshua's stall. Her father's face was solemn. Iris slowed her run. He held out his arms to her and she walked into his embrace. The veterinarian stood next to them. He took his pipe out of his mouth and said, "Iris, Joshua was an old horse. He stayed alive as long as he did because you took such good care of him."

Iris peered into the dim stall. Joshua laid on his side like he had last night, only he didn't lift his head and look at her. She walked into the stall, patted and rubbed his forehead. She knew he liked that. Then she looked at her father, "Oh, Daddy! Oh, Daddy! What will I do?"

Her father asked, "What would you like to do?"

"May we have a horse funeral," she asked. "Can we bury him on the farm?" Her legs felt like they were going to collapse. She leaned against her father. He held her tight. "I know Oscar would help us. I have to call Oscar," she added.

Her father released her. "Go inside. Call Oscar. Joshua was his friend, too."

Her mother held the kitchen door open for her. Iris walked in and said, "I can't tell if my face is wet from rain, or crying. I'm going to call Oscar. Would you call Julie and Lars?"

When she called Oscar's house, his father answered. Iris told him that Joshua had fallen asleep and died while she was at school. Would Oscar come over after school?

Oscar's father, a man of very few words, said, "Oscar will come. I will bring him."

Iris went upstairs and closed her door. She sat on her bed. Her lungs seemed to swell, and she could hardly get her breath.

She breathed through her mouth and her chest heaved, but a full relaxing breath did not come. There was a knock on her door. She called out, "Who?"

The door opened a crack, and Merry and Martha Rose peeked through.

"Come in," said Iris. "Close the door."

The girls came in. Merry stood by the door, but Martha Rose threw herself at her big sister. Iris smoothed her sister's unruly hair with numb fingers. She held up her hand and said, "I can't feel a thing."

Merry said, "Julie, and Lars are coming."

Iris slumped on her bed with Martha Rose in her lap. "I said good night to him last night. I patted him and rubbed him, and, and. . . . "

A metallic clatter made Iris turn to the window. It was Lars throwing his bike down.

Her mother called up the stairs, "Iris, Lars is here."

Iris pushed Martha Rose aside and said, "You can cry for both of us," then went downstairs.

Lars held his canvas case in one hand and a sketch in the other. His pale hair was plastered to his head. "Iris," he said, out of breath. "Look!" He held out the sketch of Joshua that Iris had chosen for him to send to France.

Iris' shoulders fell.

"My mother sent the wrong sketch to France!"

Iris took the black and white drawing in her hands and sat in the kitchen chair. She laid it on the table and looked at her friend. "Joshua died while we were in school," she said in a level voice.

Her mother took Lars' wet jacket and handed him a towel to dry his face and hair.

"No!" he blurted. "No! That's why mother sent the wrong one. You are supposed to have this."

Iris' mother said, "All the sketches were exceptional, Lars."

"I had to get Joshua right, not for the competition, for Iris!"

Iris looked at the sketch. Joshua looked back at her. He

seemed to say, “What took you so long? I’ve been waiting all day.”

When Julie and Oscar arrived, Iris and Lars were sitting at the table, the portrait of Joshua propped up by a loaf of bread. Each of them had a thick slice of buttered bread on a plate in front of them. Julie’s eyes brimmed with tears. She knelt in front of Iris, put her head on her friend’s knees and sobbed. “Oh, Iris, I can’t believe it!”

Julie’s mother came into the house with her apron still on. She walked over to Iris’ mother and said, “I believe my Julie was as attached to that fine animal as your family is. Is there anything we can do?”

Iris’ mother shook her head. “It hasn’t sunk in. Iris hasn’t cried.”

Mrs. Gonner shook her head, “She will. In time she will.”

Oscar stood a distance from Iris, his usually animated hands hanging at his sides. He asked, “Are you going to let the vet take him, or are you going to bury him?”

Iris looked at him. “What should I do, Oscar? What should I do?”

Her father and Earl came into the kitchen. Her father had his hands in his pockets. “Joshua belongs to this farm. Let’s keep him here. I’ll get Luke to help, and Earl wants to pitch in, too. We’ll need all the shovel handlers we can get.”

Julie said, “Mother, Daddy has shovels at home. Let’s get them.”

“You stay here,” her mother answered. “I’ll get shovels and your father.”

Iris asked again, “Can we have a funeral for a horse?”

Julie looked at her friend. She wiped her eyes and said, “Joshua was more than a horse.”

“I’ll get a prayer book and paper,” said Iris.

“Do you think we could sing,” asked Lars.

“Every service has singing in it,” said Iris.

"Oh, I wish my family could be here," said Lars.

Mrs. Gonner said, "I'll fetch them on my way back from the house. They'll have to sit in each other's laps."

"They're used to that," said Lars. "Thank you, Mrs. Gonner."

An hour later, Iris, Julie, and their mothers sat at the kitchen table. Annie Carlson held Benjamin in the rocker in the living room, singing him to sleep. Iris wrote out a burial service. She heard the scrape of shovels and voices as the men worked at the dirt behind the barn.

"Let's see how they're doing," suggested Iris to Julie.

Julie followed her friend out of the house, down the drive to the barn, but they didn't go in. Cookie stood in front of the barn door. "Look, Iris, Cookie's the sentry!"

Iris' father had taken off his jacket, and piled dirt on one side of a wide hole. Lars and Earl sweated and wiped their hands on their pants. Oscar stood in the grave shoveling dirt over his head. Gunther Carlson turned his hat in his hands, staring into the hole.

Luke stepped up, "I'm rested, Earl. Let me have a turn."

Iris moved in front of him. "No Uncle Luke, let me." She took a shovel from Earl and jumped into the hole. "I'll work from here," she said.

She lifted a load of dark soil and heaved it onto the growing pile. Rocks scraped against the shovel and made shivers down her back. She and Oscar worked together. Iris looked up at her father, "Daddy, how will we get him here," she asked.

"We'll pull him on a canvas tarp and drag him. Iris, come out of there now. I'll jump in."

"No, Daddy," said Iris. "I'm not done." She continued to lift, heave, lift, heave. She heard her Oscar's heavy breathing. It reminded her of Joshua's breaths the last night she sat with him.

Her father climbed into the grave and took the shovel from his daughter. "Why don't you and Julie get a sheet. We can put it over Joshua. We're almost done."

Gunther Carlson reached a hand down to her and pulled her out. She looked into the grave. "Did I do that," she asked bewildered.

At Iris' request, her mother came down the stairs with a clean sheet. On top of it was her Easter bouquet of silk roses her husband gave her the first Easter they were in Harmony. She said, "I want to put these with Joshua."

Iris looked at her mother, whose eyes were full of tears.

Iris picked up the sheet and the paper with prayers printed on it. She walked out the door and saw the barn door was open. Mrs. Gonner directed the men how to place the horse on the canvas tarp. She turned to Iris. "Here, let me have the sheet," she suggested.

Iris' mother asked if she'd like to see Joshua one last time, but Iris said, "No. I saw him after school."

Her father and Uncle Luke came out of the barn with ropes over their shoulders. Slowly the white-draped figure of Joshua appeared. Earl and Oscar pulled ropes attached to the back of the canvass. Gunther Carlson and his children followed. Cookie walked was the last in line. Iris noticed the clean swept path behind the horse.

Merry, Martha Rose, and Lily came out of the house. Mrs. Gonner walked in front guiding the men and talking to herself. "My, my, what a burden. What a sad, sad burden."

Joshua lay at the edge of the grave. Iris opened the red book to the place she'd marked and cleared her throat. Earl took off his hat and threw it on the ground. Iris began, "Into your hands, O merciful Savior, we commend your servant, Joshua."

She looked up, and her mother smiled encouragement. "Receive him into the arms of your mercy and everlasting peace." She handed the book to Julie. Gunther Carlson's eyes were closed and his lips moved soundlessly.

Julie looked up from her prayer book, raised her head and recited,

"The weight of this sad time we must obey,

Speak what we feel; not what we ought to say.
The oldest hath borne most: we that are young,
Shall never see so much, nor live so long.

Uncle Luke spoke up, "Shakespeare, always perfect." He looked at the group beside him. "A little bit of King Lear. Julie, you chose well."

The men took the ropes and guided the awkward bundle into the grave. Once the horse was settled, they struggled to pull the canvas from under his body. When they had, Iris' father turned to her, "I think you should go inside. We'll cover him. It'll take a while."

Iris' mother tossed her silk bouquet to Iris who threw it into the grave near Joshua's head. She turned around to walk away, until she heard the sound of Earl's harmonica, "Amazing Grace, how sweet thou art." After that Uncle Luke began to sing, "All things bright and beautiful, all creatures great and small, all things wise and wonderful, the Lord God loves them all."

When Iris entered the house she was astounded at how dark it had gotten. She looked at her hands. They stung.

Julie looked at her friend's blisters. "You've ruined your hands!"

Laughing Sky took Iris' hands in hers. "The ointment that healed your father's hands will heal yours. I'll run to the cabin. Julie, keep an ear out for Anna. She's asleep on the sofa." She turned to Laura Ellen. "Where are the muslin strips you bound Horace's hands with? I'll need them."

Mrs. Gonner and Annie Carlson helped set the table. There was going to be a crowd. Laura Ellen set out a ham, cabbage slaw, rolls, and green beans. Coffee began to perk on the stove. When her father and friends came in, Gunther walked over to Iris. He spoke in Norwegian. Lars stood next to him and translated. "My father says he does not have enough words, English or Norwegian, to express his thoughts. His heart is full."

Iris reached up to hug the tall man. He took her by the

shoulders and looked in her eyes. His were red. He shook his head, then bowed it, and put it on her shoulder. Iris held on to him for a long time.

Her uncle patted Gunther and Iris on their shoulders. He spoke to her, "I don't expect to see you in school tomorrow, Iris. Your hands will hurt like heck, and you won't be able to write for days."

Iris looked up at him. "I'm coming to school."

Laughing Sky entered with her leather medicine pouch. She said, "Everybody eat. I'll finish Iris' hands and we'll join you."

Oscar stood nearby. "I'm not hungry. I'll help."

"You're always hungry," Iris said.

"Not now," he answered.

Laughing Sky looked at Iris and said, "I have to clean your hands. This will sting." She submerged Iris' hands in a pan of warm water.

"Ahh!" Iris let out a yelp. Her eyes burned with quick tears.

After her hands had soaked, Laughing Sky dabbed them with a cloth until the raw skin was ready for the ointment. Oscar sat close to Iris. He put his hand on her shoulder when Laughing Sky began to bandage them. He said, "Almost done, Iris. You're brave. You're the bravest girl I know. I've said that before."

When Iris, Oscar, and Laughing Sky walked into the dining room, her father pulled out a chair. "Sit here," he said. Iris put her hands in her lap.

"I'm going to feed you," said her father. He took a piece of ham on a fork and said, "Open wide."

Those were Ben's favorite words. From his spot at the table he clapped his hands and crooned, "Ope - Wiiiiide!" He smacked the table top with his hands and yelled, "I, I, I, I," his name for Iris.

Laughing Sky stood behind her. "You'll need your bandages changed daily. I'll come after school, or you can walk over. I'll help you stretch, too. If you don't, those blisters will heal and your hands will look like claws."

Her father responded, "I remember stretching." Laughing Sky had healed his hands last winter. He said, "Dr. Brenna gives his approval to Laughing Sky's remedies. I saw him in town when my hands were bandaged. He said he'd learned as much from her as he did at medical school."

"Oh, he did not," said Laughing Sky.

"Yes, he did. He has great respect for your work."

"We learn from each other," she said.

Luke picked up Anna. She snuggled her head into his shoulder. He turned to Ben, "Sorry, little one, Anna's halfway to dreamland. You'll see her tomorrow. You are her best friend, you know."

Ben babbled, "Nan-Nan."

Iris looked up at her uncle. "See you in school," she said.

"If you insist. You'll be waited on hand and foot."

Oscar and his father got up from the table to get their coats. There was a commotion of good byes. Oscar leaned next to her and whispered, "I'll be here tomorrow, too."

All Iris wanted was to go to bed. She held out her helpless hands and said, "Mother, would you help me put on my nightgown?" She looked at her half-full plate and said to her father, "I'm not hungry."

"That's all right. You will be tomorrow. Today has been too much for everybody."

Her mother picked Ben up from his highchair and sat him in her husband's lap. "He's all yours," she said.

Ben patted his father's cheek, "Papa Daddy," he said. Then he put his thumb in his mouth.

Chapter Nine

MAY

The farm animals missed Joshua. Cookie stood in front of Joshua's stall, turned around, settled, sighed, and waited. War Bonnet stared into the empty enclosure next to her. When Iris came into the barn after school, the brown and white pony got twice as much attention. Muffin and Biscuit, Martha Roses' cats, stayed away. They never liked the barn. Too many big feet. Merry's sheep, Snowball, liked to be in the fenced yard where there was grass to eat.

Iris sat on the dirt floor of the barn and leaned against Joshua's stall. She closed her eyes and imagined the big horse snuffling behind her. When she opened her eyes she saw a man walk into the barn. The doors were closed. He walked through them. She sat up. He ignored her. He had on overalls, and turned a straw hat in his hands. She'd seen her father do that. She said, "Hello," and the man turned to her, fading from sight.

The barn door opened and her father walked in. "Iris, are you missing your old friend," he asked. Before she could answer he continued, "This is a good place to sit."

He sat down next to her, leaned against the stall, and closed his eyes.

"Don't close your eyes," said Iris. "I did, and when I opened them I saw a ghost."

Her father smiled. "Only one?"

"One. He wore overalls and turned a straw hat in his hands like you do."

Her father was still. Then he turned his head. "Say that again."

"I . . . ." she began.

"Iris, that was your grandfather!"

"What was he doing here?"

"What do you think? Checking up on things, I guess." Her father looked left and right. "Wish I'd seen him."

"I think you have to be here by yourself," said Iris. "That's when ghosts show up, when you're alone."

"How many have you seen, so far, ghosts, I mean," asked her father.

"Two. I saw Oscar's mother in my room, and now grandfather. I thought that was grandfather because he turned his hat in his hands."

"You saw Oscar's mother in your bedroom," repeated her father.

"Yes. I had a nightmare, and Oscar told me his mother used to tell him to turn his pillow over and punch it, and he wouldn't have the nightmare again. I did it, and it worked. The next morning she was in my chair, and then faded away like grandfather did. It was like they got erased."

"Have you told your mother?"

"No, just you because you came in right after your father did. You just missed him."

"Iris, you're special. I know that. It comes to me often, how special you are. I should speak up and tell you." Her father stood up, and reached his hand down to help her up. "Let's go in."

Iris hugged her tall daddy for a long time.

School would soon be over for the summer. She and Oscar would ride their ponies to their special place. Iris loved the big rock where they sat. The Lady Slippers would bloom in June. This was the only place Oscar talked about his mother. Iris wished she could share the wild flowers with Lars, or his father. Merry would love them, too. Their mother bought pads of paper for her at the hardware store.

Iris thought Merry was getting pretty good at drawing. Once Iris drew a horse, and her mother thought it was a map of the United States! Iris wasn't sure what she was good at. She loved to read. She liked to look at art books. She liked to write letters. She couldn't get a job doing anything she liked to do. She wrote in the journals Uncle Luke gave her each Christmas. She couldn't make a poem to save her life. She couldn't even knit. She didn't like to cook.

Iris opened her hands, blisters healed, no scars. Her palms were tender, though. Her mother made her wear gloves when she rode War Bonnet. When spring came, she'd ride a lot.

It snowed four inches May first. Disgusting! It melted in a few days, but everything was soggy. Iris missed seeing Gunther Carlson in the field painting near her house. Lars said his father sketched and worked outdoors as well as indoors now, but the Carlsons lived too far away for Iris to see the artist at work. Lars' entire family rode bicycles. There were eight bicycles in the barn! Annie Carlson was trying to turn the dirt in a former garden space. Iris' mother told her it was too early. The ground was frozen below the surface.

Late on Thursday, almost dusk, Iris day-dreamed the afternoon away. Maybe she slept. She could hear her mother in the kitchen with Ben and Martha Rose. She stretched. What was she doing in bed?

She got up, went downstairs and into the kitchen. There was a clank outside, and three loud knocks on the door. Her mother opened it and Lars burst in. He said, "I did it! I won! I'm going to France! Mother sent the wrong sketch, and I won!"

Iris' mother threw a dish towel in the air. "Lars! You'll put Harmony, Minnesota on the map!"

Lars rushed to Iris and grabbed her by the arms. "I won!" He kissed her soundly on one cheek, then the other.

Iris was frozen in place.

Merry came in, "What's going on?"

"Lars won the art contest," said Iris. "He's going to France."

"Can you talk French," Merry asked.

"Oui, oui, mademoiselle," he answered with a bow.

Merry continued, "When do you leave? How're you going to get there?"

Iris turned to her sister. "That doesn't matter. Lars won. That matters!"

Merry smiled at Lars. "Tell me how you did it. I want to go to France."

Lars said, "You don't have to go to France. You've got one of the best artists anywhere living here. My father will teach you. All you need to do is be in the room with him while he's working, and you learn."

Merry looked at her mother. "Do you think I could? This summer? Oh, Mother, say 'yes.'"

Her mother looked from Lars to Merry. "I'll ask Gunther. If he says, 'yes,' I say, 'yes.'

"Oh, Mother, if Mr. Carlson will teach me, my life will never be the same!" Merry waltzed away. She called over her shoulder, "Congratulations, Lars!"

"I'll tell my father to expect you."

That wasn't the end of the art excitement at the Andersen house. On the way through the hall at school two weeks before summer vacation, Iris saw several pictures framed and lined up on the wall. One had a blue ribbon on it. There was Cookie! Merry had sketched him sleeping in front of Joshua's stall. Iris could almost see the dog's ribs rise and fall with her breathing. Merry had done that? Iris hadn't paid much attention to Merry's drawing. She drew a lot, but Iris never asked to see her work.

During the summer, Mrs. Ludvigson planned come over two afternoons a week. She'd read with Martha Rose, and begin to teach Merry and Martha Rose French. Merry was determined to go to France. Iris didn't have plans for the summer. Their mother would take Merry to the Carlson's one afternoon a week. Her mother would stay for a visit with

Annie. Merry would watch Mr. Carlson work.

The end of May was loud! Uncle Luke and Laughing Sky's new home began to take shape late in the month. Digging, hammering, and sawing was going on all the daylight hours. A path was worn to the site. The house would be like the cabin Laughing Sky lived in, one long room across the front. This living space stretched from one end of the house to the other. The kitchen was in one corner, Uncle Luke's big dining table and four chairs would fit. His bookcases would be there, lining the back wall of the room. The end opposite the kitchen would hold Laughing Sky's loom and yarn bins. Uncle Luke's desk would not be far away. The desk would be situated in front of a window that looked out over her father's fields. There would be a lot of windows. Two wood stoves stood at each end of the room. Laughing Sky planned to weave rugs to place in front of chairs. She and Uncle Luke were looking for a large rug to cover most of the floor under the table and chairs.

There'd be a loft, like the cabin. Anna's room would be up there. Luke and Laughing Sky's room would be downstairs. They had a well dug, and the pump for the kitchen was ready to go. The outhouse was built first. It wasn't like any outhouse Iris had seen! The floor was made of stones, and the inside was painted yellow and white. Iris had never seen an outhouse painted inside. There were high windows on two walls. This was a sunny bright outhouse. Unheard of! Earl, Oscar, Mark, Lars, Mr. Crocker, Iris' father, and Uncle Luke spent every afternoon digging the house's foundation. The neighborhood would gather for the roof-raising. Uncle Luke and Gunther Carlson worked together when Luke wasn't building his house. Mr. Carlson promised to paint it.

Greenfield Lutheran, was going to have a picnic at Goose Lake. This was the lake Martha Rose didn't get to visit last May when her friend drowned. Iris guessed that people needed time, and Pastor Nilsen decided Greenfield Lutheran would bless the water with their presence. Iris and Julie's mothers were on the picnic planning committee. Martha Rose had ideas for games in the empty pasture nearby. Oscar wanted to have a horse race. Iris thought that would be fun. The picnic planning committee thought otherwise. Iris said she wanted to ride War Bonnet anyway. The horse needed some activity. They had never done any racing. Oscar said that War Bonnet was young and fast. He was amazed at how well Iris handled her. After plodding Joshua, War Bonnet was a pleasure. She obeyed Iris' every twitch of feet and reins. When Iris wanted to ride, she was allowed to wear a pair of her father's old pants. Her mother had cut the legs the right length, and Iris turned the waist over and belted them to keep them on. She could climb up on that horse, and ride all the way to Virginia!

Picnic morning was bright, breezy, and blue. Martha Rose looked outside and said, "Not too hot. Not too cold. Just right."

Iris' family drove to the lake. Oscar would ride his pony, Blue, and lead War Bonnet. Earl would ride his horse, Drink.

Iris would never forget the day Laughing Sky's brother, One Deer, gave her War Bonnet. That happened at a picnic, too.

One Deer had lived up north on a reservation for a year. Iris missed him. He was a lot like her Uncle Luke, tall, strong, and respectful. The more she thought of him, the more she missed him. She sat in the back seat next to a window. Martha Rose was in the middle, and Merry, by the other window. Minnesota needed rain. Dust flew in the car windows.

Goose Lake lay like a great blue plate. No dragon flies. No mosquitoes - yet. The Andersens parked in the pasture, and walked towards tables set under trees near the shore. As usual, there was enough food to feed an army of Vikings. Iris spotted Earl. Oscar couldn't be far away. The horses were tethered a good distance away, and drank from a creek that fed into the lake. Iris walked over to greet War Bonnet. She stroked his neck, "Hello, good girl. How was your trip? Did you behave?"

Oscar walked up. "She was gentle as Merry's lamb, I mean sheep. When are we going to ride?"

"After lunch, I guess," said Iris. "Look. Your father, Uncle Luke, and Mr. Crocker are at it already." The three men stood together talking and using their hands to measure how wide or narrow some board needed to be. "Can't they ever stop working?"

"Not my dad," said Oscar. He looked up. "Pastor Nilsen is ready to say the blessing. Let's go."

Pastor Nilsen raised his hands to the sky, looked up, and said, "Thank you, Father for this perfect day. Amen." He turned to the crowd and said, "I'm speechless at the beauty of this gathering." He looked at his wife and their adopted daughter, Elsa. Elsa had her arms wrapped around her mother's neck.

The crowd laughed and repeated, "Thank you, Father, for this perfect day! Amen!"

Iris and Oscar grabbed plates. The oldest went first. They finally got to the food tables. Oscar loaded his plate. Iris asked, "Are you sure you can carry that?"

His response, "I'm always hungry."

"I've noticed," said Iris.

Oscar's father sat with the Andersens. "Well, Miss Iris, when's the race start," he asked.

Iris looked at her mother. "I don't think there is a race."

"I saw your horse. She looks bored," he said.

Oscar chipped in, "Yeah, she's ready to run!"

Iris' father winked at her and said, "I'd like to see you ride, Iris."

Her mother rolled her eyes. "Iris has on a dress."

"I brought my pants just in case."

This time her father blinked both eyes. "I think we ought to have a little trial, don't you, Earl?"

"Oh, I don't want to get in trouble with the ladies, but a short run wouldn't hurt."

"No betting," said her father.

"No sir-ee," said Oscar's father. "Just once around the parking area. Then we can take out the canoes."

"Great idea," said Oscar.

Iris looked at her mother. "Please?"

Her mother squinted her eyes, "Once."

Iris reached up, took Oscar's hat and snugged it on her head. "I might need this."

She changed into her baggy pants in the car. Her father led War Bonnet from under the trees. The horse looked lazy. Oscar rode Blue, and behind him came his father on Drink. To everyone's surprise, Bobbin Frye rode up on his pony, as well as two farmers, Bobbin's father, and May's father, Mr. Rhoades. May was the reason they were here at Goose Lake. She'd drowned here last year.

There was a great hoot from the guests as riders made a circle around the cars. Iris heard folks holler that she never thought would raise their voices. Mrs. Ludvigson was there in her purple hat and scarf. She waved her scarf in the air and said, "Ride 'em, Iris!"

Iris raised her eyebrows. Her mother stood in front of the circle of folks. She wasn't smiling.

Her father said, "Let's ride around once, then meet here. Pastor Nilsen, you give them a 'ready—set—go—and they'll circle two times 'round. That all right?" he asked the riders.

"Yes!" they shouted together.

Iris was in a horse race. She first sat on a horse two years ago. She'd never even raced Oscar. She had seen races. She'd been to county fairs in Virginia as well as Rochester. She thought about how the riders looked then, and drew her knees in, bent over, and gathered the reins. The horses trotted the made-up track once, then gathered to wait for Pastor Nilsen's "Go!"

Earl and Oscar jumped ahead immediately. Bobbin, his dad and Mr. Rhoades were in a little group, and Iris got a 'feel' from War Bonnet. She ducked low and said, "Whatever you want to do, little girl, do it!" War Bonnet understood English. She took off. The brown and white pony dodged past the threesome, and overtook Oscar and Earl in a heartbeat. Iris heard Oscar yell something. Oscar's hat flew off and her hair blew back. War Bonnet's mane was in her face as Iris leaned into the curves. The first round was done, and Iris couldn't hear horses behind her. She leaned forward and said, "It's all yours, girl!" and War Bonnet clicked her speed up. Iris and her Indian pony waited at the finish line for the other riders to appear. She looked around. Farmer's hats were flying in the air. Her mother's eyebrows arched, and her mouth was open. Iris saw Mrs. Ludvigson's purple hat float through the air.

Pastor Nilsen came up to her and grabbed War Bonnet's harness. He stroked the horse's neck. "Well done, little girl, well done." He looked up at Iris and laughed. "You must be as surprised as the rest of us. None of us knew a city kid could ride an Indian pony like you do. One Deer will want his horse back."

"Oh, no! War Bonnet is mine," answered Iris.

Pastor Nilsen said, "I'm just kidding. Don't let anyone buy this animal from you. Folk's will try."

Oscar jumped off Blue and ran to help her dismount. Iris said, "I can do this," as he reached for her.

"Let me help anyway. I'll get to put my arms around you."

"Oscar!" said Iris as he put his arms up to her. He helped her to the ground and did hug her, right in front of everybody.

He said, "Heck, Lars kissed you! Merry told me. I can at least hug a winner! I never saw you ride like that. You keeping a secret from me?"

The pick-nickers began to gather around Iris. Her father grabbed her by the shoulder. Her mother stood behind him, eyes shining. Mrs. Ludvigson waved her scarf at Iris. Martha Rose and Merry stood nearby with their mouths open. Oscar's father, Bobbin, and the two other riders walked over with their horses trailing behind. Mr. Rhoades said, "Looks like we have a pro in our neighborhood. Where's Dr. Beard, did he see this?"

Just then Dr. Beard, Harmony's veterinarian, walked up to Iris. "I guess you never got a chance to do that with old Joshua.

I never saw this filly run like that. This is going in the history book. A girl beat the four best riders in Harmony. Make that a girl and an Indian pony. Yes sir! History."

Iris didn't like the idea of a 'girl' winning to be a big deal.

The last week of school would start tomorrow. What would Uncle Luke think of next? Her classroom was a mess. Desks were not in order. Friends sat together. Uncle Luke sat on a stool in the middle of them. He drew pictures on the board. One thing he insisted on was that each class member have a reading partner. It didn't have to be someone in class. Iris and her mother were partners. They read Nancy Drew mysteries and talked about them. Iris's favorite was Lilac Inn. They had finished re-reading Peter Pan.

Iris' mother had read to her and her sisters since Iris could remember. Before Martha Rose was born, she and Merry used to get in bed with their mother for bed time reading. Sometimes her mother drifted off, and the book slipped from her hands. The girls would giggle, slip out of bed, and go to their room. Iris still sat on Martha Rose's bed when her mother read one of her favorite books. Now her mother was reading Peter Pan to Martha Rose. Martha Rose decided she wanted a night light like Wendy, Michael and John had, so her mother put a candle in a glass hurricane lamp. Martha Rose wanted to fly, too. Then she said she wanted a horse that could fly, and would name it Peter Pan. In Richmond, Iris' mother had sat on the front porch and read to the girls. The next thing you know, four or five neighborhood children would join them. Mother read Bible stories from a big red Bible. Now she and Iris ventured into fiction, and sometimes poetry. Iris loved poetry best. She and her mother finished a book of Emily Dickinson's poems in April. Uncle Luke owned a copy, and Iris and her mother took turns reading to each other. Iris would try to imitate Miss Dickinson in her own poems. She didn't have a favorite 'Emily' poem. There were too many, but one she'd memorized was # 737.

The Moon was but a Chin of Gold
A Night or two ago –
And now she turns Her perfect Face
Upon the World below –

Her Forehead is of Amplest Blonde-
Her Cheek - a Beryl hewn –
Her Eye unto the Summer Dew
The likest I have known –
Her Lips of Amber never part –
But what must be the smile
Upon Her Friend she would confer
Were such her Silver Will –

And what a privilege to be
But the remotest Star –
For Certainty She takes Her Way
Beside Your Palace Door –

Her Bonnet is the Firmament –
The Universe - Her Shoe –
The Stars - the Trinkets at Her Belt –
Her Dimities - of Blue–

Iris loved the moon, too. Here in Minnesota it seemed close enough to touch. In the fall it turned pumpkin orange. She wrote a poem for Uncle Luke about the moon.

Here it is.

THE MOON
Iris Andersen

Tonight my moon is Silver
I think that I will Sleep—
And let her shine her radiance

and know that She will leap
into my room, into my dreams
and peaceful will I keep.

Iris was embarrassed to share it. Her mother loved it. (Her mother loved everything Iris wrote.) Uncle Luke was honest. His response was, "A good start, Niece. Emily would be happy."

Iris took her journal and began a new poem:

I cannot see my friend but know he's there
His shadow's in the barn dusk
His scent is everywhere –

She put her pen down. The ink blotched as she leaned over her book. Tears streamed onto the page. Grief put words in her mouth.

Chapter Ten

JUNE

Iris had never seen anybody kiss like that! Uncle Luke took Laughing Sky in his arms, pulled her to him, and they kissed. It went on and on. They didn't see Iris and Oscar. They didn't see anything. They were buried in each other. Iris shook her head at Oscar, turned around and hurried home. They would come back later.

Oscar said, "It is their first anniversary." His face was dark red.

Iris felt the heat of her own face. She kept her distance from Oscar as they walked home.

When they entered the kitchen, her mother asked, "Where's Anna?"

Iris and Oscar were supposed to bring Anna back to the farm. Her mother was going to take care of her while Laughing Sky and Uncle Luke went on a trip.

Oscar looked at Iris. Iris' mother looked at their faces. Iris began, "Umm . . ."

"It's all right, Iris. I'll get her after lunch. The love birds will have plenty of time to drive to Rochester for their second honeymoon," said her mother. "At least this time they won't have Anna with them."

Iris said, "We couldn't . . . disturb them."

"I have plenty for you two to accomplish this afternoon," her mother began.

"Oh, Mother, Oscar and I are going to see if the Lady Slippers have bloomed."

"That's too bad. Lars and Merry are going to sketch today. I know Lars will miss seeing you both. I hoped you two could spend some time with Martha Rose."

Oscar looked at Iris. Iris looked at Oscar. He said, "Maybe they could come with us and sketch the Lady Slippers."

Iris' eyes opened wide. "Oscar, that's our place!"

"It's time to share," he answered. "Time to share."

"But Oscar . . . Oscar . . . " Iris could feel her voice rising. "We were going to ride together."

"Lars can ride his bike. Merry can ride with you."

Iris' mother asked, "What about Martha Rose? I'm going to Annie's with Ben and Anna today. Is there any way Martha Rose could join you?"

"Oh, Mother, can't Martha Rose go with you," Iris asked.

"I heard that," a voice from the living room carried into the kitchen. "You want Oscar to yourself. You won't let anybody have him. You won't let anybody come to your flower place. I'll run away. Go! I won't be here when you come back. Promise!" Martha Rose stamped up the stairs to her room.

Iris called after her, "Martha Rose, what are you doing? Come back."

Her sister yelled, "I'm packing!"

Oscar hid a grin, but Iris' mother laughed out loud. "Iris, your sister means business. Could you take her with you?"

Oscar cut his eyes at Iris. "We will, Mrs. Andersen. We'll take them all, Merry, Martha Rose, and Lars."

"Oh, Oscar," wailed Iris. "I was looking forward to this."

He replied, "I still am!"

Lars arrived on his red bicycle. His father rode behind him on his black bike. Both had satchels slung over their shoulders. When Lars saw Oscar he yelled, "Oscar! I didn't know you were going to be here. Glad to see you!"

Oscar yelled back, "I didn't expect you, either. You're in for a surprise."

Iris rolled her eyes.

Oscar took Mr. Carlson's bike and leaned it against the porch. "I am glad to see you," he said, and shook Gunther's big hand. Iris thought Oscar was going to bow.

Iris' mother came out on the porch, "Ah, the crowd grows. Should I send a basket of food? Welcome, Gunther. You and Lars are in for Lady Slipper surprise."

Gunther looked confused. Lars spoke in Norwegian to his father. Gunther raised his eyebrows and said, "Ja! We go!"

Merry and Martha Rose came out of the house. Merry had a satchel, too. War Bonnet was saddled. Oscar never used a saddle on Blue. Oscar lifted Merry up to sit behind Iris, and he lifted Martha Rose up on Blue's back. Lars and his father mounted their bikes. Oscar cried, "We're off!"

Iris' mother stood on the back porch and waved. Martha Rose clung to Oscar with one arm, but saluted her mother with the other. "We'll be back," she called. "Goodbye, goodbye!"

The two horses walked at a fast pace, but the cyclers kept up with them. Neither horse seemed to mind being followed by the red and black bikes.

Iris remembered when Merry had ridden with her and her father two years ago when the tornado tore the school roof away. Merry was squeezing her just as hard now.

"Merry, why do you squeeze me," Iris asked.

"I thought I was supposed to," her sister answered.

"You need a pony of your own," said Iris. "Then you won't squeeze me!"

Merry said, "A pony of my own . . ."

When the crowd arrived at the creek, Oscar and Iris tied up their ponies, and Lars and his father propped their bikes against a tree. Oscar announced, "We walk," and signed two walking fingers with his right hand.

Mr. Carlson grunted, "Ja. Valk," and he switched his first and second fingers together.

Iris thought maybe sign language would be the best way to communicate with Mr. Carlson. Oscar was a genius.

The group entered the special place in silence. The trees parted, and in the open space sat the large boulder. Iris climbed to her favorite perch. She looked at the space around her. Yes!

The Lady Slippers were in bloom. Their heavy pink slippers danced in the sun.

Lars took out his satchel as if it was lunch, and he hadn't eaten for five days. Merry stared at the flowers. She let her satchel fall to the grass. Mr. Carlson walked close to a bloom, fell on his knees, and began to speak in Norwegian. Iris thought he was praying. She looked at Lars.

He said, "My father has seen orchids in Norway, but this, nothing like this. He is saying, 'the face of innocence, the face of joy.' He gets sentimental. Watch him."

Martha Rose had climbed next to Iris who took her in her lap. Merry continued to stare, while Lars and his father took their sketch pads out and began to work. Gunther Carlson sat cross-legged in the grass close enough to the bloom of an orchid as if he wanted to smell it. He didn't look at his sketch, only the bloom.

He said something to Lars who asked, "How long will they be here?"

Oscar answered, "About two weeks."

Lars relayed this information to his father who replied, "Ja. Ve come each day."

Lars shrugged his shoulders and asked, "Oscar, may we?"

"Oh, yes, yes! My mother would be happy to have you." As he said this his eyes were bright.

This was not like any visit Iris remembered. She wanted Oscar to herself. She had to share her horse, the Lady Slippers and Oscar. She heaved a great sigh.

Merry took her sketch pad and sat in the grass. She held her pencil in one hand, the blank pad in the other. She looked at Lars and his father, making broad strokes on their paper. She looked at the blooms. She looked at her page, and said, "I can't." She closed her pad, and laid back on the grass. "Look at the clouds," she said.

Iris held Martha Rose close. Soon her little sister was

breathing quiet long breaths. She had fallen asleep. Oscar sat at Iris' side. "My mother used to hold me like that. I think I remember it. I fell asleep." He put a hand on Martha Rose's head. "Mother used to stroke my head. I remember that." He stroked Martha Rose's short bangs. "Yes. I remember." He looked Iris in the eyes. "I'll remember this, too."

Merry sat up, took her pad and pencil from her satchel, shaded her eyes, and began to draw clouds. Iris thought they looked like they were drifting across the sky. She looked at her sister crouched in the tall grass. Merry's legs looked like they'd been stretched. Her bare arms were thin, white and long. She had tied her thick blonde hair behind her in a lazy pony-tail, off-center. She always wanted her hair off-center. Her nose was longer than it had been. Iris sat across from Merry at every meal, but hadn't looked at her. She did now. Her sister wasn't a child anymore. She was growing beautiful.

The artists worked in silence. Martha Rose slept. Oscar let his hand slip from her head to Iris' hand. He took it in his, raised it to his lips, and kissed it. Then he let their two hands rest on Martha Rose's shoulder. Iris could not look at him. She looked at their clasped hands.

Oscar whispered, "I'm glad you're here." He looked at the preoccupied artists. "They're welcome. I have a feeling . . . Iris, are you listening?"

She raised her head to him, "I am."

"I have a feeling this is right," he said.

Gunther Carlson's Lady Slippers appeared in Mr. Crocker's hardware store. They appeared in the Minnesota Institute of Art, and the Chicago Art Institute. They were shipped to Florence, Italy, Oslo, Norway, and Bremen, Germany. Two weeks of painting, sketching, and drawing resulted in twenty-eight finished canvases. Lars completed six sketches. Merry drew five cloud scenes. She took them home and used pastels to finish them. Mr. Crocker hung one of Lars' pictures, and one of Merry's next to Mr. Carlson's. He said he would make frames for any picture that needed one. He made them of cherry wood, or birch. Gunther Carlson said they were as fine as the artwork in them.

The month of June passed in slow motion, except for when Iris and War Bonnet took to the dirt roads around Harmony. No slow motion here! Iris' hair and War Bonnet's mane and tail flew behind them. Farmers stopped their tractors to watch. She and her horse understood each other. Her mother finally set her free. She didn't have to take a sister or brother with her. She was on her own. When she and War Bonnet returned from their rides, they were covered in sweat and dust. Iris walked her pony, brushed her, bathed her, and shared a secret.

Chapter Eleven

JULY

Iris and War Bonnet had a secret. They'd take off down dirt roads every morning before the sun got too hot. Iris didn't mind the heat in Harmony as much as she did in Richmond. It was humid in Richmond. She could wring her clothes out by eleven a.m.

Why are Iris and War Bonnet working out? I'll tell you a secret. They're going to race in the Fillmore County Fair. (Don't tell anyone.) Iris is going to wear pants. She will be the first and only female to take part. She made up a name so no one will know she's a girl. On the official race form, she's going to call herself Anders Strauss. She'll say she's seventeen years old. She'll lie. She doesn't care. She plans to wear one of Oscar's hats. She hid one he wore the last time he visited. She would braid War Bonnet's mane and tail.

The county fair was lively. Iris' mother and father agreed she could show War Bonnet in the horse competition. Farmers and a couple of veterinarians would walk past and feel the horse's legs and check their teeth, stuff like that. There was a building filled with a quilt show, pie competition, blacksmithing, wood turning, Scandinavian chip carving, and a butter sculpture. AND there was food, cheese curds, fried walleye, potato salad, lemon bars, and early corn on the cob. Each church had a tent set up with tables. Greenfield Lutheran was serving coffee, milk and deserts. Mrs. Ludvigson was there waving her apron to fan herself. Mrs. Nilsen held Elsa in her lap. The two-year old was asleep. Mrs. Gonner cut brownies and bars and placed them on paper plates. Julie helped. Even she had no idea what Iris was up to.

The races started after lunch. There was a children's race,

then the big one. Iris recognized every horse in the stable. Harmony was a small town. Everyone would see War Bonnet, but no one knew her plan. Iris wore a light blue blouse and dark skirt. When it was race time, she'd go to the lady's tent and change into pants and her barn boots. She was ready. War Bonnet was ready. Iris was certain.

Oscar and his father stood by the corral talking about saddles and saddle soap with Iris's father. Oscar climbed up on the corral fence and gave his pony half an apple. He handed the other half to Iris. "For War Bonnet," he said.

Iris couldn't look him in the eye. She was afraid he'd read her mind. "Thanks," she said. "I'll give it to him as a treat later." She put the apple half in her pocket.

"What are you going to eat for lunch," Oscar asked.

"I'm not hungry. I'll wait 'till I get home."

"That could be a long time, Iris."

She said, "Don't worry about me." It sounded harsher than she meant it to.

Oscar walked away. "I'm going to eat," he said. "Come on, Dad." Oscar took his father by the arm.

One o'clock came. The little children lined up on their ponies. Iris didn't know which was cuter, the children or ponies. The riders were all boys, of course.

The gun went off, and the ponies jumped and jumbled together. The boys hollered and kicked their boots against their pony's sides. They made a lot of noise. One pony began to eat grass. No matter how much the boy yelled or waved his hat, that pony was going to eat grass. Nope, not running. The boy began to cry, and his farmer father came over, lifted him off the horse, and led the pony from the field, boy in one arm, horse following. The other ponies trotted and straggled around the track. They would go around twice. Iris couldn't tell who was in front. The ponies had decided to stay together. The crowd began to laugh. Iris hoped they wouldn't laugh at her! At the last gasp, Bobbin Frye's little brother's pony pulled ahead by a nose. Iris was glad he'd won. Bobbin would be talking about this for a long time.

As fathers led ponies and children away, Iris slipped off to the women's tent. She took off her dark skirt, and shoes, and put on her old pants and boots. She pushed her hair up under the hat she had 'borrowed' from Oscar. Then she leaned down and got a handful of dirt and smeared it on her cheeks and hands. She ducked her head, left the tent, and walked into the corral. War Bonnet snickered. Iris said to her, "Nothing's funny. Let's get to work." She put her foot in the stirrup and swung herself up.

She walked War Bonnet to the back of the pack. So far, so good. Earl Runs Like Fox and Oscar were up in the front. Mr. Rhoades was there, and Bobbin's father. There were about fifteen horses in the race. Iris kept her head down. As she heard the count begin she heard a familiar voice say, "Hey!" It was Earl, Oscar's dad. The gun-shot sounded and they were off. Iris kept her eyes on the track, and talked to War Bonnet. "Take your time, girl. Take your time. I'll let you know when to let loose. That-a-girl. Real smooth."

Iris and War Bonnet began to move up in the pack. They riders would circle the field five times. By the third time around, Iris was two horses away from the lead. Oscar was in front, and Bobbin Frye's father just behind, and Earl Runs Like Fox third. Iris didn't give War Bonnet his head yet.

She pulled ahead of Earl and Mr. Frye on the fourth circuit of the track. Oscar looked back. He sat straight up in his seat and said, "Iris!" In a heartbeat, Blue stumbled, tried to make up for it, but fell. Oscar went over the horse's head. The crowd was hollering, "Go! Go!" but Iris couldn't. She pulled War Bonnet to a halt. The horse heaved and jittered to stay in the race, but she pulled him close to Blue, and slid off. Oscar did not move. Blue tried to stand up, but couldn't. Dr. Beard and her father ran to the field. Oscar's Dad slipped off of Drink, and kneeled next to his son. The race was stopped. Dr. Beard felt Blue's feet and ankles. He concentrated on Blue's right ankle. He looked at Oscar's father, "It's bruised, but not broken."

Iris knelt down next to Blue and began to cry great heaving sobs. "I'm sorry, I'm sorry, I'm sorry," she wept. There was no movement from Oscar.

Dr. Brenna hurried over. "Don't move him," he warned. He felt all over Oscar, his legs, arms, chest and head. "He's knocked his breath out, but I don't feel any broken bones."

Iris took 'her' hat off and threw it on the ground." It's my fault, my fault," she said. "It's my fault!"

Her father's shoulders drooped. "Iris! You were on War Bonnet?"

"Oh, Daddy," Iris dropped her head and her father put his arms around her. "I wanted to race so bad, now look!"

Her father said, "You were about to win!"

"Oscar will hate me forever," Iris said.

Her father answered, "I doubt that."

"When Oscar looked back and recognized me, it startled Blue."

A crew of men came with a stretcher for Oscar. He was limp as a new puppy. Dr. Brenna put Oscar in the back seat of his car. Earl Runs Like Fox got in the front.

Her father said, "Let's go, Iris. It's time to go." He held his big girl close as they walked away. There was a crowd in front of them. Her father said, "Let us through, please, let us through."

Iris looked into the silent crowd. Lars stared at her. His whole family must be here. Iris remembered her dirty face. Her mother pushed through the people and grabbed her. "Oh, Iris, what made you do such a thing!"

"She wanted to race real bad, Laura Ellen," said Iris' father. "Let her be for a minute."

Mrs. Ludvigson stood at the edge of the crowd, "Great ride, Iris! Great ride!"

Gradually the crowd began to chant, "Great ride! Great ride!"

Iris blew her nose on her father's handkerchief and tried to say ‘thank you’, but she couldn’t mouth the words. She hid her face in her father’s side.

Mr. Rhodes rode up and said, “Horace, I’ll take Earl’s horse home.”

“Thanks, Randy,” said her father.

Iris had never heard Mr. Rhodes first name. He was May’s dad. May was dead. Joshua was dead. Her grandfather was dead. Blue and Oscar were injured. She’d never, ever, ever, ever, make it up to Oscar. Never.

Iris got in the back seat of their car. Her mother found her skirt and shoes in the lady’s tent. Her sisters got in on either side of her. Her mother drove back to the farm, and her father rode War Bonnet. The ride home was awful. Iris cried. Merry cried. Martha Rose sobbed, “Oh, poor Oscar, poor Blue,” until her mother said, “Martha Rose, that’s not helping.” Martha Rose began to hic-up.

Iris put her head in her hands and covered her face. She said, “Mother, I’m sorry. I will never ride a horse again. I’m going to give War Bonnet to Oscar.”

Her mother replied, “Oh, no you won’t. Oscar may ride War Bonnet, but he was a gift from One Deer to you. Iris, I know it seems like the end of the world, but Dr. Brenna says Oscar is going to be all right. Blue will recover. It’s the way things happen in this world. This accident was not your fault.”

“It was too!” said Iris louder than she’d planned. “I wanted to ride like a boy, but I’m not a boy! Oscar was so surprised to see me that he jerked and Blue fell. It is all my fault! Let me get out,” she said. “Stop the car. Let me out! I’ll walk!”

Her mother sighed. “Iris, we’re going home. I’ll let the girls out, then you and I are going to l to see how Oscar’s doing. Your father will be along soon. He can get Ben from Luke and Laughing Sky’s cabin. You and I are going to check on Earl and Oscar.”

Iris’ sisters were quiet as they got out of the car and walked into the house. Their mother went in with them and turned on the lights. She came back to the car and got behind the wheel.

"Let's check on our friends," she said.

When they arrived at Oscar's house, Dr. Brenna's car was out front. Laura Ellen knocked at the screen door, and Earl hurried to open it. He said, "He's awake, sore, and asking for you, young lady." He nodded to Iris.

"Me?"

"Come in."

Iris and her mother followed Earl into the living room. Dr. Brenna sat next to the sofa where Oscar laid. He tried to sit up when he saw Iris, but Dr. Brenna put his hand on his shoulder to keep him from rising. Oscar had a wet towel on his forehead, a line of blood dripped from it.

Iris fell on her knees near Dr. Brenna. "Oscar, I would never have raced if I thought this would happen."

Oscar looked at her, "You almost beat me," he mumbled.

Dr. Brenna commented, "Yes, she did. You'll have a re-match soon. They called the race, so there were no winners."

Iris said, "I won't ever do that again!"

"You're good on a horse, Iris," said Dr. Brenna. "You're a natural. It would be a shame for you not to give War Bonnet her head. That is one fast horse. When One Deer gave her to you, didn't he tell you she was the fastest horse on the reservation? This is what that horse has been dreaming about!"

"Dr. Brenna, no. One Deer didn't say anything about racing. Oscar, you ride War Bonnet in the re-match."

"I don't need to ride War Bonnet. You had on my hat!"

"I'll give it back."

Oscar raised himself a little, "You looked great!"

Dr. Brenna stood. "This young fellow needs a couple days rest. Earl, I mean rest. No horse riding, no field work. I know you have plenty to read here," her looked at Oscar. "Maybe I'll ask for a book report to keep you down."

"I'll keep him down," said Earl. "I'll keep him in bed and play my harmonica day and night."

Oscar smiled, "Oh, not your harmonica, Dad."

Iris' mother spoke up. "Iris and I will be over first thing in the morning. I'll bring breakfast, and she can read to you, Oscar. You do need to be still. Do you like Blueberry muffins?"

Earl said, "Oh, Mrs. Andersen, Oscar and I will be just fine. No need for you to come all this way . . . "

Laura Ellen said, "Earl, you live ten minutes from our farm. I'll be here with Iris. I'll bring Horace, and you two can work on Blue's ankle."

Iris looked up at Oscar's father, "You can't stop my mother. You know that. See you in the morning. Goodbye, Oscar. I'm sorry."

"Don't be sorry," Oscar said. "I'm proud of you! Fillmore county won't forget that race for a long time . . . or the re-match."

Chapter Twelve

AUGUST

On the first of August, Iris walked into the kitchen. "It's hot, Mother. Are the windows open?"

"Yes. Every window in the house is wide open. It isn't humid, but it is certainly warm this morning." She pulled out Iris' chair. "I'm glad it is just us this morning."

Iris looked at her chair. There was a box in it. "What's that," she asked.

"It's something for you. I hope you like it."

Iris opened the box. It had been a shirt box. Inside was folded gray fabric. Iris had no idea what it was. She picked up the fabric, and a pair of slacks unfolded themselves in her hands. They were her size. Underneath was a vest. "Mother?" Iris began.

"I want you to be comfortable when you ride. I asked Annie to make the slacks and vest for the race."

"Annie made me riding slacks?" Iris raced upstairs, "I'm gonna' try these on!"

"Iris, wait a minute. I want to ask you something."

Iris stood in the doorway.

"When I was with Annie, I asked her to come over this week, and walk from room to room, starting with your room, and give us ideas about making this house feel like our house. You're the first one I've told."

"You haven't told Daddy?" asked Iris.

"I wanted to have a conversation with you first."

"May I have a conversation in my slacks and vest?"

"Of course, change in the bathroom so you won't have to go upstairs."

"I'll do it, but I don't have to think long about your idea.

Mrs. Carlson will listen to us, about what we like, then she'd be full of ideas. I can't wait! Oh, everything is happening at once." Iris took her new outfit into the bathroom. The slacks fit. They were perfect, length, and waist. The vest was the final touch. Iris pulled her hair back. When she put on a hat, she'd look like a boy. Who would think that Iris Andersen had a pair of racing pants? She would write Dorothy tonight.

Iris and her mother sat at the kitchen table, a pad of paper for ideas in front of Iris. She said, "I need to be in my room to think about this. I'll be back with a list of ideas.

She went up the stairs to her room. Her furniture was from Virginia. It had been her mother's when she was a girl. She sat on the twin bed. The walls in her room were white, dull white. She could make out spots where pictures used to hang. When they'd first moved in, Iris' windows were bare. Now, over her two long window were sheer curtains, and on top, heavy drapes. She couldn't see out of the windows. Her father said that drapes kept out the cold. She got up and pulled the drapes aside. Her windows looked into the yard. Iris stood on a blanket chest, and took the heavy draperies down, rods and all. Then there were the sheers. She took them down. She looked out. Heck, she could see half of Fillmore County from her window. The sun came in like, well, like the sun should! Her walls looked worse in the light. She held the sheer curtain up to the halfway mark on the window. That was enough curtain! She prowled her room. She wanted it to be bright. Winter was dark for a long time. She'd repaint her walls white, real white. She'd paint the dresser deep orange, and her bed? Turquoise! She would cover the blanket chest with a quilt. She could see her room. Her desk would be . . . . yellow! Mrs. Carlson was an inspiration. Iris couldn't wait to tell Julie.

She ran downstairs. Her father was in from the barn. He blinked at her and grinned. Then she remembered. Oh, yes. She had on slacks and a vest. She held out her arms, "Look at me!"

Her father scratched his head. "Hmm," he mused. "I thought I had three girls and one boy. . . . "

"Daddy!" said Iris.

"Come here. I'm going to squeeze you 'till you yell like a girl."

Iris darted around the table.

"Horace," her mother shook her head. "What has gotten into you this morning?"

"This young filly here. Look at those long legs and yellow mane. I'd buy a horse like that!"

"Oh, Daddy," said Iris, scurrying off. "I'm going to win that race, and give you the prize money."

"Don't be so quick to speak," her father said. "You just might like to spend one hundred and fifty dollars."

"I don't need one hundred and fifty dollars," said Iris. She turned to her mother, "I do know what I want to do in my room, though."

"Write it down, and we'll give it to Anna this afternoon. She and Lily are coming today to put our heads together about the picnic. It's late to plan, but we know where it will be at least."

"At Laughing Sky's cabin, right," asked Iris.

Her father answered, "Yes, and the race will be on the road from town out past the creek."

"How far is that," asked Iris.

"About four miles."

"Daddy, tell me what you'd do with one hundred and fifty dollars. I am going to win it, and give it to you!"

"I know someone who one hundred and fifty dollars would make real happy. Someone who needs transportation."

"Are you talking about the Carlsons," Iris asked.

At that moment, Merry and Martha Rose walked into the room rubbing their eyes. Martha Rose's mother had cut her hair an even length just below her ears. It was a mess this morning.

Iris suggested, "Martha Rose, get your brush and let me help your scrambles."

"I like my scrambles," said Martha Rose.

Her mother said, "Let your sister help you. You don't want

to be a scramble head all day, do you?"

"I do," said Martha Rose, hunching her shoulders.

Mrs. Carlson and Lily came after lunch. Iris still had on her slacks. "I'm going riding this afternoon," she explained. She added, "I love these slacks. I could wear them all day!"

She gave her list to Mrs. Carlson and held her finger to her lips so her color choice would remain a secret. Mrs. Carlson read the list, and her eyebrows swept up to her bangs. All Mrs. Carlson said was, "I can't wait to get started! Monday, it is."

"Monday! That's four days," said Iris. She turned to her father, "We need to go to the hardware store and buy paint."

Mrs. Carlson said, "I'll get the paint. You can pay me for it, but I want to mix these colors myself."

Iris noticed Mrs. Ludvigson sitting between Oscar and his father in Greenfield Church on Sunday. Whenever Mrs. Ludvigson leaned over to whisper to either of them, her big hat brim bumped them. She whispered in church a lot, no matter who she sat next to.

At one point, Mr. Runs Like Fox turned and looked at the woman next to him, a long steady look. On the way out of church, Oscar caught up with Iris.

Iris said, "Mrs. Ludvigson sat with you today."

"We're going to her house for lunch," said Oscar.

"She's never sat with you before," said Iris with her eyebrows raised.

Oscar answered, "That's right." He continued, "Iris, I need to ask you something."

Iris could see her parents and sisters standing by their car. Her father had sleeping Ben in his arms. They waved at her. She waved back.

"I need to go," she said.

Oscar put his hand on her arm. "I need to ask you a question," he repeated.

"Iris, will you be my girl?"

"Oscar!" Iris pulled away. "Is that your question," she asked.

"Do you want to be my girl, or not," Oscar asked.

Iris said, "Do you want me to be?"

"I think you already are," answered her friend.

Merry walked up the steps from the parking lot. "Are you coming," she asked. "Daddy wants to know if you want to walk home."

"I'm coming," said Iris.

Oscar said, "So, what's your answer?"

"You said it. I already am!" Iris leaned over and kissed him once on the cheek.

"Let's go, little sister. What are you waiting for?"

Iris hopped in the back seat of the car. "I'm Oscar's girl," she announced.

Martha Rose shot back, "Yeah, but you're not gona' marry him."

Because the picnic was at Laughing Sky's cabin, Iris felt she had lived this event before. Uncle Luke and his family had moved into their new house behind the barn, so the cabin was empty. The windows and doors stood open. Church tables stood on the porch. They were filled with food, the same food as two years ago: fried chicken, ham, hot dish, macaroni and cheese, corn, corn, corn, lemon bars, potato salad, and chocolate cake.

There was one huge difference. Iris wore her slacks. When Mr. Crocker saw her he yelled, "Hey, look at you!" Mrs. Ludvigson did a twirl, blushed, and said, "Uff-da, Iris!"

There was her father's favorite Norwegian word, "Uff-da." Her father said it when he lifted something heavy, when Cookie tracked mud in the kitchen, when her mother plopped Ben in his arms for a diaper change. It wasn't a word her mother used. Her mother called it "leftover Norwegian."

Iris heard Martha Rose whistling. A whistle from Martha Rose meant she wanted to talk to you. Iris found her.

"This is for you," said Martha Rose. She had a small squashed sunflower in her hand.

"Well, thank you," said her big sister.

"If you keep this yellow flower, you will win the race, okay?"

Iris studied her sister. "I'll put it in my vest pocket," she said.

"Now you're the winner!" The little girl held her hand out to her sister. Iris took it and gave it a shake.

"Pshew, now I'm not worried," Iris said with a sigh.

Iris watched Mr. Rhoades lead two ponies to a post near Laughing Sky's porch. One was a chestnut brown filly with a white patch on her forehead, white "socks" and tail. The other pony was smaller, all white. Iris' father walked over to Mr. Rhoades, and was soon deep in conversation. Iris' father called Merry, and Iris watched as her father lifted her sister onto the white pony's back. Merry on a pony? Merry was skittish in the barn. When she rode behind her big sister, she squeezed her so hard Iris could hardly breathe. Merry reached for her father, not to be lifted off, but to give him a good hug. Her father shook Mr. Rhoade's hand, then led Merry to her mother. This was too much to miss. Iris called, "Merry, you're on a pony!"

Merry hollered, "I know I am. This is my pony. It used to be May's. Her name is Snow White. May named her, and that's what I'm calling her."

"We can ride together. I'll teach you how to saddle her and brush her . . . "

"I'm not saddling her. I'm riding bareback," said Merry stroking the filly's neck.

"May wanted Martha Rose to have this pony, but Martha Rose wants a bike." Merry blinked and a tear trickled down one cheek. "May was Martha Rose's best friend, but my friend, too."

Merry's father lifted her from the pony and held her close. "Iris wants to help you a little."

Merry reached for Iris who put her arms around her sister.

Iris looked around for Oscar. She wanted to tell him Merry's news. There he was with his father, adjusting Blue and Drink's harnesses. There was also Mrs. Ludvigson. She had a plate full of food. She'd never eat all that! Oscar's father took the plate from her, and began to fork potato salad in his mouth. He was all smiles, rare for Mr. Runs Like Fox. Mrs. Ludvigson was flamboyant and talkative. Earl, well, Earl was somber, and nodded his head instead of speaking. Oscar was a lot like him, a man of few words. Laughing Sky said it's the Indian way to be in the world. She called it respectful. Earl Runs Like Fox and Lois Ludvigson were a study in contrast. They were like kite and string: Mr. Runs Like Fox, the string, and Mrs. Ludvigson, the kite.

She seemed to fly about in her skirts, hats, and veils! Iris noticed the two mis-fits were together often, like last Sunday in church. She'd have to talk to Oscar.

After the meal wound down, Pastor Nilsen stood on Laughing Sky's porch the way he had two summers ago. Gunther Carlson appeared next to him. When the group noticed them, they quieted, Pastor Nilsen began, "Brothers and Sisters in Harmony, the impossible has happened. Lutherans and Catholic are breaking bread together!"

The crowd laughed. Father Leo waved to the group from the edge of the crowd.

Pastor Nilsen continued, "The Carlsons are ours. We claim them and bask in their fame. Gunther Carlson has put Harmony, Minnesota on the map, and his son, Lars, is about to do the same."

Cheers rose from the crowd.

Pastor Nilsen waved his arms. "Gunther has something to say."

The crowd quieted. Mr. Carlson turned his cap in his hands and began to speak.

"*Mange takk*, Thank you." He put his big hand over his heart. "My life is come back. I am hope. No, I am home.

Home. *Tusen takk. Tusen takk.*"

Everyone clapped their hands and shouted back, "Tusen takk!"

The artist's family joined him on the steps. They were a crowd all by themselves.

Then Pastor Nilsen raised his arms and declared, "We have a race to finish!

Riders, mount your horses!"

www.ingramcontent.com/pod-product-compliance
Lightning Source LLC
Chambersburg PA
CBHW070344130626
46556CB00007B/3016
* 9 7 8 1 6 3 0 6 6 2 0 9 7 *